# RAINBOW SUMMER

## Sarah Franklin

ATLANTIC LARGE PRINT

Chivers Press, Bath, England.
Curley Publishing, Inc.,
South Yarmouth, Mass., USA.

Library of Congress Cataloging-in-Publication Data

Franklin, Sarah.
  Rainbow summer / Sarah Franklin.
    p.  cm.—(Atlantic large print)
  ISBN 0–7927–0612–9 (lg. print)
  1. Large type books.  I. Title.
[PR6056.R285R35  1991]
823′.914—dc20                                 90–27321
                                                    CIP

British Library Cataloguing in Publication Data available

This Large Print edition is published by Chivers Press, England, and
Curley Publishing, Inc, U.S.A. 1991

Published by arrangement with Harlequin Enterprises B.V.

U.K. Hardback ISBN 0 7451 8112 0
U.K. Softback ISBN 0 7451 8124 4
U.S.A. Softback ISBN 0 7927 0612 9

# RAINBOW SUMMER

# CHAPTER ONE

'You look exactly like a marigold in a rainstorm!'

Katy Lang looked up, though she knew perfectly well who was addressing her. That cool voice with its attractive hint of Scottish brogue was all too familiar to half the nurses at St Anne's—not least to her. She avoided the amused dark eyes and grunted:

'Thanks!' pulling her cloak closer round her and lowering her bright head against the spring shower as she hurried across the hospital forecourt.

Sean MacInnon, St Anne's resident paediatrician fell into step beside her, his white coat flying open and his thick, dark hair falling over his forehead. 'Cheer up. The exam results will be out any day now. Next thing you know you'll be holding the exalted position of Staff Nurse and it'll be fourpence to speak to you!' He smiled. 'If you're very good I might take you out to dinner to celebrate. How would that appeal to you?'

Katy turned to him, her green eyes flashing fire. 'It would be more like a punishment if you really want to know! Why should you imagine that going out with you would be such a treat?'

He shrugged unconcernedly, looking more

1

amused than before. 'Well, I can't say I've had any complaints so far!'

She turned away. 'I'm sorry, I'm on duty in five minutes. I have to go.' And without a backward glance she flung away in the opposite direction.

In the cloakroom she took off her damp cloak and tried to mop the rain from her auburn hair. Already the little tendrils that had escaped from her neat chignon had curled themselves into tight corkscrews and nothing she could do would persuade them to lie flat again. She saw what Sean had meant by a 'marigold in a rainstorm'. She looked a fright, she told herself disconsolately, and for the fourth time that morning she opened her bag and took out the letter. It had arrived that morning by the first post. Tracy and Sonia, her flatmates had been on night duty, so she had been alone when she had opened it. There had been one for each of them too, but she felt certain that theirs didn't contain the crushing news that hers did. She slumped into a chair, staring again at the words—still hardly able to believe it was actually happening to her. Three years of hard training and study, culminating in that nerve-racking exam—and all for nothing. She had failed. Of course it would be that multiple choice paper they had been faced with in the afternoon. She was sure that her essays had been good. In fact she had put so much into them that she had worn herself out both mentally and physically—which was probably the reason for her failure. She swallowed hard at the lump in her throat and blinked as a tear rolled helplessly down her cheek. Now she was about to go on duty and hear all the excited success stories. She would have to smile and say 'congratulations' at least a dozen times and pretend that she wasn't green with envy and sick with shame. How would she bear it?

Despairingly she wished her mother were still alive so that she could ring her and have a good moan—get it out of her system. But now there was only Dad—sweet, vague Dad who was really only interested in his garden and his work at the research laboratory.

Katy pinned on a fresh, clean cap and peered at herself in the mirror, dabbing at her nose with a touch of pressed powder to hide the shine. Better get on up to the ward or she'd have Sister after her. She was on the children's ward and there were three post-operative cases, so today would be busy. She may not be a Staff Nurse yet but she was still needed.

As she pushed open the swing door she saw Sister Blake glance at her watch and a protest rose to her lips. Surely she couldn't be more than a couple of seconds late?

'When you take your coffee break, Nurse Lang, I'd like to have a word with you in my office,' Sister said, then added, 'Don't look like that, child. I'm not about to eat you alive!'

Almost immediately Katy was up to her ears in work. There was the little girl transferred from the burns unit after skin grafts; the seven-year-old boy who had had the tonsillectomy; the appendix emergency who had come in yesterday afternoon and the suspected skull fracture. Katy worked hard, only too aware, as she went about the routine tasks, of the subdued excitement of the three other nurses who had taken their exams at the same time as her.

'You're keeping very quiet, Katy—' The question was coming at last. 'Didn't you get your results this morning too?'

Katy straightened up from the bed she was making and looked the other girl in the eye. There was no point in beating about the bush. 'Yes—and I failed,' she said bluntly, relieved that at last the hateful words had been spoken. The other girl looked shocked.

'Oh no! I'm sorry, Katy. Have you told the others?'

In no time at all the whole ward knew and Katy had to endure their well-meaning sympathy which was almost worse than the disappointment, so much so that she was almost glad when her coffee break came round and it was time to report to Sister's office. Tentatively she tapped on the door and

4

heard the brisk instruction to enter. Carefully she closed the door behind her and turned to face the desk. Sister Blake smiled.

'Come and sit down, Katy.' On the desk was a tray of coffee and two cups. Sister opened a drawer and took out a tin with a picture of Windsor Castle on the lid. Opening it, she offered it to Katy. 'Here, have a chocolate biscuit.'

'Thank you.' Katy took one, her green eyes looking speculatively into Sister Blake's brown ones—trying to assess their mood. They looked compassionate.

'I've heard of course,' she said at last. 'And I'm sorry.'

Katy bit her lip hard. It would be unthinkable to weep in front of Sister Blake. 'But not—surprised?' she whispered.

Sister poured the coffee and handed her a cup. 'Well, now that you've said it yourself—no, not altogether. It will have been the theory—the multiple choice paper. Your practical assessments were excellent and I'm sure that your essays will have been perfectly adequate. But when it came to theory you were always too anxious to get back to your patients. Still'—she smiled brightly. 'Only another four months to wait. Concentrate on your theory during that time and I'm confident you'll pass with flying colours next time.'

'No!' Katy heard herself say. 'I'm not

5

going to take it again. I couldn't face it.'

Sister Blake sighed. 'I know how you feel this morning, but it will pass. You're not the first, you know, and you certainly won't be the last. You're a very good nurse, Katy, especially with children. In fact I was going to have a talk with you this morning even if you had passed, to try to persuade you to try for your RSCN. I feel sure it's what you're cut out for.'

Katy still felt the lump in her throat. 'If I can't make SRN I wouldn't make that either,' she said despondently.

'Look, why don't you have a word with the Senior Nursing Officer when you go off duty? I'm sure she'll help you all she can and that she shares my view of your abilities.' Sister held up the coffee pot with a questioning look. 'More coffee?'

Katy shook her head. She felt her throat was too constricted to allow anything to pass down it. All she wanted was to be alone and wallow in the morass of her own misery, but there was little chance of that. As soon as her break was over it was time for the doctor's round and she would have to endure the spectacle of Sean congratulating the other three nurses, watching their simpering and the sickening way they played up to his already inflated ego. Katy ignored him blatantly; attending to the needs of the patients, her eyes averted from his gaze even when he addressed her personally.

She ate her lunch in the canteen, sitting alone, tucked away at an out of sight corner table, her mind racing with impulsive plans. She would go home and keep house for Dad. That was the obvious thing to do. She had some leave due and if she gave in her notice today it would be almost up by the time she got back. Dad was hopeless at looking after himself and the never-ending series of cleaning women he had had since he had been on his own had all failed miserably at making the house feel like the home they had enjoyed when her mother had been alive. Each time she went there she saw the lovely home her mother had created falling further into neglect. The more she thought about it the more she was convinced that she was making the right decision. She would hand in her notice first thing in the morning.

As she was leaving the hospital, another April shower began, pattering down heavily on to the forecourt flower beds, making the earth smell damp and fresh. She was running for the gates, head down, when a hoot from behind made her spin round crossly. Sean MacInnon's bright yellow sports car was inching along behind her. She stopped as he drew level.

'Hop in.'

She shook her head stubbornly. 'No thanks.'

He leaned over and opened the door. 'Don't be such an idiot, girl! You're getting soaked.'

Reluctantly she climbed into the car and slammed the door. He sat looking at her thoughtfully, the engine still running. 'Look, Katy—I'm sorry about the facetious remark I made this morning. I didn't know about—you know. Come and have a drink—let me make amends.'

She lowered her head so that he wouldn't see her chin wobbling. 'I can't go anywhere looking like this.'

'You look all right to me, but if it's your uniform you're worrying about we could go to the Swab. They're used to it there.'

The 'Swab and Scalpel' was the nickname for the King's Head, a pub round the corner from St Anne's. It was where all the younger doctors, nurses and students gathered in their free time to entertain, celebrate and exchange news.

Katy sat glumly in a corner waiting for Sean to get her a sherry from the bar. Out of the corner of her eye she could see once more the hated corkscrews hanging over her forehead and she could feel them against her neck. She looked a perfect fright and wished fervently that she could have escaped to the flat and shut herself away in the bathroom where no one could see her despair.

Sean returned with two glasses, seating

8

himself opposite and looking at her with disturbing intensity. He was tall and broad-shouldered—Katy guessed in his early thirties. Everyone said he was quite brilliant. Why is it, Katy mused, that some people seemed to have everything going for them whilst others had nothing? Sean MacInnon had looks, money and a staggeringly clever brain whilst she, on the other hand, had none of these things. Life just wasn't fair. From what she had managed to gather during the course of the day she was the only student nurse to fail her finals—except Mandy Gail, the giggling dumb blonde whom everyone had expected to fail anyway and who was getting married next month in any case. Being put on a par with Mandy had made her feel worse than ever.

Sean pushed the glass towards her across the table. 'Come on, drink up. It'll do you good.' He took a long pull at his beer. 'So, what are the plans now?' he asked conversationally.

She took a sip of the sherry and felt slightly better. 'I'm going home,' she told him simply.

He nodded. 'I mean after that.'

'That's it. I'm going home to stay.'

The dark eyebrows shot up. 'Giving up, you mean? But everyone says you're a very promising nurse.'

'Well, everyone is obviously wrong,' she

said boldly. 'My mother died two years ago and ever since then my father has been struggling alone. He needs me and it's beginning to show. It seems the obvious thing to do now that I've failed.'

He frowned. 'How old is your father?'

'Forty-eight,' she told him gravely.

He laughed. 'Good heavens, I thought he must be at least eighty by the way you were talking about him. Of course he doesn't need you. He's probably quite glad to have you off his hands!' He leaned forward. 'Look, Katy, if you're really set on giving in your notice at St Anne's I have an idea that might interest you. Why don't we have dinner together tonight, then I can tell you about it?'

She shook her head firmly. Deep inside her she admitted the idea of having dinner with Sean MacInnon was exciting, but she knew it was not for herself he was asking her. At best he was only trying to make up for the tactless remarks he had made that morning. Perversely she refused point-blank: 'Not interested.'

'How do you know that when I haven't told you anything about it?' he enquired, his dark eyes twinkling. Leaning forward he touched her hand, making her nerve-endings tingle. 'You must admit that this evening's going to be pretty miserable if you're going to sit around feeling sorry for yourself. Surely it would be a whole lot happier for you if you went out.' He leaned back, regarding her. 'Go home and put your posh frock on. I'll take you somewhere really swish. You'd like that wouldn't you? Go on, admit it.'

Her chin went up and her eyes narrowed suspiciously. 'Just what is all this in aid of?' she asked him. 'After all, I'm not exactly your type, am I?'

The corners of his mouth twitched. 'And just what *is* my type? What makes you think you know it?'

She blushed furiously. 'What I mean is that there must be some reason other than—' She was getting herself into a mess. 'That there must be something in it for you,' she ended lamely.

He chuckled and gave her hand a squeeze. 'Well now—that would be up to you, Katy, wouldn't it?'

She bit her lip as she looked into the mocking eyes. 'I meant—I thought—' She looked at her watch. 'Heavens! Is that the time? I have to go now. No, don't get up. I can catch a bus at the corner.'

He caught her wrist. 'I'll pick you up at half-past seven.'

She tried frantically to escape but he was holding her fast, his eyes serious now as they looked into hers.

'I said half-past seven, Katy. I want to tell you about this idea of mine and if you turn it down then, well, fair enough. I mean it.'

11

'All right then,' she said meekly.

He let go of her wrist and she elbowed her way through the crowds, glad to allow them to swallow her up. Outside she gulped at the fresh air. Within her chest her heart thudded unevenly and her wrist still tingled from his grasp.

At the flat Tracy and Sonia were getting ready to go on night duty. The first thing they asked her was the one question Katy had been dreading. When she broke her news to them they looked at each other in dismay.

'Oh, what rotten luck!' Tracy said at last. 'We were both so sure that you'd have passed too.'

The 'too' told her that they had been lucky in their results and she shrugged resignedly. 'So you've passed. I thought you would. Congrats!' She went through to the kitchen to make herself a cup of coffee and the two girls looked at each other helplessly.

'What are you going to do with yourself tonight, Katy?' Sonia asked. 'You won't hang around here brooding, will you? Why don't you take yourself off to the cinema?'

Katy lifted her head. 'As a matter of fact I'm going out to dinner with Sean MacInnon,' she announced casually. There was a stunned pause as the girls took in this remark and Katy smiled to herself. Their shock took some of the sting out of the day's disappointment. Sonia was the first to

12

recover.

'When did this happen? When did he ask you?' she asked.

'Oh, when I had a drink with him on the way home this evening. He gave me a lift.' Katy was enjoying herself. Both Tracy and Sonia had masses of boyfriends and although they were kind to her they sometimes seemed a little patronising. No need for her to tell them about the idea he wanted to discuss with her.

Sonia laid a hand on her arm. 'Look, love, I'd go carefully if I were you. Sean has—well, a bit of a reputation, and you—'

Katy turned and looked her in the eye. 'What about me? I'm silly and inexperienced, is that what you were about to say?'

Sonia coloured. 'No need to be so touchy. I was only trying to warn you!'

Sonia had come to nursing later than most. She was twenty-seven and knew her way around. Sometimes her 'woman-of-the-world' attitude irritated Katy and as she turned back to the boiling kettle on the stove her cheeks flushed a deep pink. Tracy stepped in:

'I'm sure Katy can look after herself, can't you, love?' she said kindly. 'And Sean can be very sweet when he wants to. I think it was very nice of him to invite you out tonight.' She smiled and patted Katy's shoulder. 'What were you thinking of wearing? Is there anything of mine you'd like to borrow?'

'According to you two he's either being kind or he wants to seduce me! I can't see any reason to dress up for either of those, can you?' Katy's eyes flashed their green fire and the other two girls looked at each other.

'Well—I suppose we asked for that,' Sonia said. 'Come on, we'd better get a move on, or we'll be late.' And without another word they left.

Katy sighed and chewed her lip. If only she didn't flare up like that. The Irish temper she had inherited from her mother would get her into serious trouble one of these days. Tracy and Sonia were only trying to be kind, she told herself. Except that they always made her feel like a backward child when it came to the opposite sex. She drank her coffee and thought objectively about what they had said, remembering that Sonia had been quite keen on him at one time, until something had happened to put her off. Katy could hear her now holding forth about him: 'He's just a playboy who likes to play the field. Anyone who gets into his clutches had better play the same game as his or prepare to be hurt!'

There were other rumours as well but Katy had always allowed them to go in one ear and out of the other. In a closed community like a hospital there were always plenty of rumours. Sean was attractive and an incurable flirt. Three quarters of the nurses in the place fancied him and there was no way that anyone who had been out with him was going to admit to a boring evening—or even a tame one.

The stories were more than likely exaggerated. Nevertheless Katy couldn't help feeling a *frisson* of excitement as she opened her wardrobe and looked at its contents. He had said he would take her somewhere 'swish', and she didn't want him to be ashamed to be seen with her. Her clothes looked incredibly dull and she wished she hadn't been so waspish when Tracy had offered to lend her something. Opening Tracy's wardrobe she peered inside. She had one or two really lovely things—like the flouncy black skirt and the little camisole top that went with it. She took them out and held them against herself. If only she could get her hair to lie smooth and sophisticated like Sonia's dark shining pageboy, or Tracy's sleek bouncy wedge. She sighed and pulled out her pins, letting the auburn mass tumble about her shoulders. Maybe with this gipsyish skirt it wouldn't matter if she looked a bit tousled.

By the time seven-thirty came around she was ready and waiting, sitting bolt upright on the edge of a chair and trying hard not to nibble her fingernails. Maybe he wouldn't turn up—or if he did suppose the girls had been right and he was the Casanova of all time. Could she handle him? Could she put him in his place without looking a complete fool? She groaned aloud. If only she had said no and stuck to it!

## CHAPTER TWO

When the doorbell rang Katy almost fell off her chair with fright. Scrambling to her feet she took a last hasty peep into the mirror. Her small heart-shaped face peered out anxiously from the mass of auburn waves. Her green eyes were huge and bright with excitement, her cheeks pink. 'I'll just have to do,' she told her reflection desperately. Why was it that she never seemed to achieve the effect she set out to? Taking a deep breath she opened the door.

'Oh—hello,' she said breathlessly.

His dark eyes flicked over her, the corners of his mouth lifting. Was he laughing at her? Did she look ridiculous after all? Involuntarily her hand went to her hair. She reached down her coat.

'I'm ready—shall we go?'

'But of course.' He offered her his arm with mock solemnity and once again she got the impression that he was amused, like a grown-up indulging a child.

'It's been quite a day. I could certainly do with a drink,' she said in a desperate attempt at sophistication. He looked at her in surprise then roared with laughter.

'Then a drink you shall have, little Katy. What will it be—ginger pop or lemonade?'

As Sean parked his car outside the restaurant he turned to look at his companion. She hadn't spoken a word since they had left the flat. Switching off the ignition he turned to her, one arm along the back of her seat.

'Well, let's have it—what did I do?' He grinned. 'I must say this makes a change. It's usually on the way home that they won't speak to me!'

She raised her eyes defiantly to his. 'If you must know, I don't like being laughed at and treated like a child,' she told him. 'I find it humiliating and I've enough humiliations for one day. I am twenty-one, you know—almost twenty-two.'

He nodded gravely. 'I'm sorry.'

'I know I'm not sophisticated like Tracy and Sonia,' she went on. 'And right now you're probably regretting the time you're wasting on me—' She bit her lip, wincing inwardly. She was doing it again—going too far. Any minute now she'd ruin the evening completely. She stole a look at him, her cheeks burning. He was smiling, this time respectfully.

'I promise to treat you with all the reverence due to an old lady of going on

17

twenty-two—how's that?'

'Well—all right.' It was no use. She'd never get the hang of handling a situation coolly.

Sean had chosen a country club on the outskirts of the town. It was quiet this evening and when Katy joined him in the bar, having divested herself of her coat and taken another panic-stricken look into the mirror, he was waiting, two tall glasses before him. He nodded towards them.

'I hope this will be to madame's taste.'

She eyed it suspiciously. 'What is it?'

'A champagne cocktail.'

'Oh!' Her cheeks turned pink as she sipped it experimentally. It was delicious and the bubbles tickled her nose, making her wrinkle it.

'Well—is it all right?'

She nodded, relaxing a little. 'It's lovely. I've never had—' she glanced at him—how naive he must think her. 'Such a nice one,' she finished. Better not to let him know just how inexperienced she was.

He leaned back and regarded her thoughtfully. 'Tell me about yourself, Katy. I've known you for a long time in a vague sort of way yet I don't really know anything about you.'

She shrugged. 'There isn't much to know. I suppose I've led rather a routine sort of life so far. School, then straight into nursing.'

18

'What about your family?' he asked. 'You mentioned your father.'

'I'm an only child,' she told him. 'My home is at Kensbridge. It's about twenty miles away—near the coast.'

'I know it well. I have an aunt there.' He grinned. 'You see, already we have things in common.'

'Dad works at the research laboratory there,' she went on. 'He's been alone since my mother died as I told you. He's one of those vague dreamy types. Sometimes I wonder if he remembers to eat.'

'And you plan to go and see that he does,' he finished for her.

She nodded decisively. 'It seems the obvious thing to do.'

'Has he pressed you to go home and keep house for him?' he asked.

She looked up in surprise. This was getting to be more like an interview than a dinner date. 'Good heavens no!' she said.

'Then don't you think you might be mistaken in feeling that's what he wants?' He leaned forward. 'Listen, Katy. I happen to know that you are a good nurse—especially with the children. Will you at least listen while I tell you about the job I have in mind for you?'

She nodded. 'I'll *listen*—but that's all.'

He took a long drink from his glass. 'Do you read?' he asked.

19

'Read? Well, yes, a bit.'

'Have you read a book called *Devil's Country*?'

'Last year's rave best-seller—yes, I read that. But why are we talking about books? I thought you were going to tell me about a job.'

'I'm coming to that. It would only be a temporary job—for the summer. If you took it, it would give you time to think and get things straight in your mind. At the end of the summer you could still go home and look after your father if that was what you still wanted—or you could go back into nursing.'

She frowned. 'What sort of job is it? Something to do with selling books?'

He laughed. 'No. I'll explain. Jake Underwood, who wrote *Devil's Country*, is a very old friend of mine. He's a widower with a small son, but quite recently he married again. The family has taken a beautiful old house in Yorkshire for the summer. Jake is commissioned to write a sequel to his book and he needs to be somewhere quiet, where the press and the public can't get at him, in order to do it. The success of his first book has been quite overwhelming. Toby—that's his little son—is eight and an asthmatic. Jake would like a girl to go with them to be a sort of nurse-companion for him while they're there.'

'What about school?' Katy asked.

Sean shook his head. 'For the past six months he hasn't been able to go to school, his asthma has been too severe. Luckily Claire, Jake's second wife, is a teacher, so she has been able to tutor Toby at home. They're hoping that the pure air up there in Yorkshire will benefit Toby too.' He smiled at her. 'It would be rather a nice job. Toby is a pleasant child and I'm sure you'd get along with the Underwoods. It would almost be a holiday for you and they're offering a good salary. Why not give it a try?'

She considered for a moment, pursing her lips. It certainly did sound interesting and tempting—but it was nursing and she had made up her mind to give that up. If she were going to carry on she might as well stay on at St Anne's. She voiced this thought and he said:

'I'm sure you're being too hasty about that too. Why don't you take time out to think about it? This would be the perfect way to make up your mind without having to rush.'

She looked at him speculatively. 'I get the distinct impression that you are in some way involved in this case yourself. Have you been treating the little boy?'

'Not exactly—but you're right, I am involved. Maybe you've heard that I'm taking a three-month sabbatical this summer?' He looked at her enquiringly but she shook her head. 'I'm doing research on the asthmatic

21

child for one of the medical journals and Toby is a particularly interesting case. I have a house in Yorkshire, left to me by my grandfather, and it was at my suggestion that the Underwoods rented a house nearby. They have agreed to allow me to study Toby for my research.'

'I see—well, I hope you find a girl for the job,' she said, drinking the last of her cocktail. It was wonderful what you could do when you had plenty of money, she thought. It seemed that everything dropped neatly into Sean MacInnon's lap.

'I don't want just any girl, Katy,' he told her, his eyes looking into hers. 'I want you.'

For a moment she was completely taken aback. Her breath caught in her throat as the devastating eyes met hers, then resentment reared its head again. It wasn't *her* he wanted. That wasn't really what he was saying at all. It was merely that she had presented him with a challenge and he was used to getting things his own way.

She drew herself up stiffly. 'If the Underwoods are doing the employing maybe they should have the choice,' she said, her eyes glinting.

He continued to look at her steadily. 'They have entrusted the choosing to me,' he said simply.

'And did you tell them that there was bound to be some stupid girl failing her finals

22

who'd jump at the chance of a job that wouldn't tax her feeble brain too much?' she demanded hotly.

He smiled calmly. 'I like a girl with spirit, but you really mustn't start getting paranoid about failing your finals, Katy. You know perfectly well that you'll pass next time if you really make up your mind to. No, I want you for this job because you have a natural affinity with children and I believe we could work together.'

She stared at him. 'Work together—how do you mean?'

He sighed. 'I would require you to make notes on the boy's progress and condition—keep a sort of diary. I believe Toby would be relaxed with you and one of the things I want to study is to what extent he is affected by tension and the removal of it.'

As he was speaking a waiter came to tell him that their table was ready. They rose and moved through to the dining-room. When they were seated and the waiter had gone Sean looked at her enquiringly.

'Well—what do you think?'

She shook her head stubbornly. 'I've told you, I've made up my mind to go home and look after my father. When I make up my mind I don't change it.' She glanced sideways at him. 'I hope you won't feel you've wasted a perfectly good evening.' She picked up the menu. 'I suppose I'd better choose something

23

cheap under the circumstances—or maybe I should pay for my own dinner?'

He snatched the menu from her. 'Katy Lang, I don't know whether to laugh at you or hit you over the head with this menu! In view of where we are I'd better just satisfy myself with choosing for you. You'll have the steak!' He summoned the waiter and ordered briskly, including a bottle of expensive wine in the already sumptuous meal. Katy's lip curled. All right, if he wanted to show off then let him! After all, she didn't eat like this every night of the week.

As they ate, Sean continued to tell her about the Underwood child in spite of the fact that she had shown no interest in taking the job.

'He first contracted asthma when he was about three,' he told her. 'He was very bad at the time and the condition affected his growth. He's still small for his age. Soon after his mother died it cleared up quite suddenly and as time went by the family almost forgot about it, then just as suddenly, about eighteen months ago, it reappeared, worse than ever. It became so bad that he had to be removed from the boarding-school he'd just started and as I explained, Claire has been teaching him at home ever since.'

Katy was thoughtful. The case interested her in spite of her refusal to become involved. 'Might it have been the school? It's quite traumatic for a little boy of that age to be sent away from home, especially after losing his mother.'

He looked up at her with a grin. 'So you're not as indifferent as you make out to be.'

'I didn't say I was indifferent,' she said hotly. 'Naturally I find it interesting, but that doesn't mean I want to take the job.'

He didn't press the point.

*　　*　　*

As they crossed the car-park the night was cool. The sky was clear and the moon had risen. Katy felt a little woozy from the champagne cocktail and the wine they had drunk with their meal, but she tried hard not to let Sean see this as they walked towards the car together. When he took her hand she made no attempt to snatch it back. Ordinarily she might have been irritated by the gesture, thinking that he only did it because it was expected of him, but the wine had softened her reasoning, simply telling her how good her hand felt enclosed by his large warm one. They drove back in silence until they reached the tall Victorian house, the ground floor of which made up the flat occupied by the three girls. Sean got out and came round the car, opening the door for her. His arm held hers firmly as they walked up the path. In the porch he looked down at her.

'Give me your key.'

She blinked up at him. 'What do you want that for?'

'Would you believe to open the door for you?' In the light from the street lamp she could see the corners of his mouth twitching and catch the glimmer of laughter in his eyes again. This time it was because of the effect the wine had had on her. She straightened her shoulders and took a deep breath.

'I'm perfectly capable of opening the door for myself, thank you,' she said with dignity.

'I can see I'm being too subtle for you,' he said. 'Don't I get invited in for a nightcap?'

She shook her head. 'You certainly do not!'

He lifted his arms helplessly. 'I see—I'm supposed to kiss you goodnight out here on the doorstep, am I?'

'You're not supposed—' She got no further. The next moment Sean's arms were round her and his lips were on hers. He kissed her briefly, then paused for a second before taking her lips again, this time pulling her close to him, his lips moving sensuously against hers. As he released her she leaned helplessly against him, her heart beating wildly.

'Mmm—you're very sweet, little Katy,' he said, his face buried in her hair. 'And I have a very strong feeling that we *will* be working together this summer, whatever you think now. When you change your mind just let me

26

know, will you?'

She closed her eyes as his warm breath tickled her ear deliciously, then suddenly she registered what he was saying and struggled free. 'Th—thank you for a nice evening and—and dinner,' she said, gulping hard. 'But I shall not be changing my mind. You'd better look for someone else for the job.' Frantically she scrabbled in her bag for her key, then thrust it into the lock and turned it, almost falling into the hall in her haste to get away from him. As she turned to close the door she caught the look on his face.

'What's the desperate hurry, Katy?' he asked lazily. 'Are you afraid of me—or is it yourself that you're afraid of?' And chuckling softly to himself he walked away from her, down the path to his car, pausing at the gate to wave and blow her a kiss. Furious with herself for standing there long enough to see it she slammed the door hard.

Inside she leaned weakly against it. Damn him! If she hadn't had all that wine she would have been able to conceal her feelings better. When he had kissed her she had felt as though her knees had turned to water. She decided that all the rumours she had heard about him were true. But if he thought he had only to kiss her to have her chasing after him to the ends of the earth—or at least to Yorkshire—then he was mistaken. She would show him just how wrong he could be. She

27

may have failed her finals but she did know
how to make up her mind and stick to it!

## CHAPTER THREE

Katy arrived at the bus stop and put down
her case with a sigh of relief. It was ten days
since she had had the shattering news of her
failure and Sean MacInnon had taken her to
dinner, and since then nothing had seemed
quite the same. All the girls she had begun
her training with were now qualified nurses
and had been busily applying for jobs. The
air had been full of plans, both for the new
jobs they were hoping to get and for the
holidays most of them were going to take
first. Sadly, she realised that even if she had
decided to stay on, things could never be the
same as before. Even the girls she knew at St
Anne's would now be far above her in status.
She felt humiliated and inferior and couldn't
wait to be on her way home. After her
fortnight's holiday with Dad she would have
only another two weeks of her notice to work
out, then it was home to all that was dear and
familiar.

The May sunshine was warm and she
unbuttoned the jacket of the grey suit she had
bought to cheer herself up. Underneath it she
wore a white blouse with a pie-frill collar and

her bright hair hung loose about her shoulders, just the way that Dad liked to see it. When she had telephoned to tell him she would be coming home for a fortnight he had sounded vaguely pleased. He had also muttered something about a new friend he wanted her to meet. She was delighted. Dad didn't have much of a social life. He had always left that sort of thing to her mother who had had no difficulty in making friends. Mary Lang had always captivated people with her vivaciousness and striking looks and she could have charmed the very birds from the trees with her sparkling personality and her soft Irish brogue. Katy sighed, wishing she could have inherited her mother's charm and beauty.

Last night the girls she shared the flat with had given a party but somehow she hadn't been in the mood. Sean MacInnon had been invited but had failed to put in an appearance. Katy imagined that he was out with someone else. Since the night he had taken her out to dinner they had hardly spoken; it might never have happened. In fact Katy sometimes wondered if she had dreamed the whole thing. When he was on his ward rounds he would smile and nod—sometimes they would pass in the corridor or see each other at a distance across the canteen. It was almost impossible now to imagine that she had actually been in his arms that night and of course it was obvious from his present attitude that it had all been done in the hope of persuading her to take the job he had told her about. She sighed and looked at her watch. Another ten minutes before the bus was due. Suddenly she heard a loud hoot and a familiar yellow car drew up alongside her, Sean's dark head leaned out of the window.

'Taxi, Miss?'

She smiled. 'I couldn't afford a taxi for the distance I'm going.'

'You never know your luck. Your destination wouldn't happen to be Kensbridge, would it?'

She stared at him. 'Well yes—but—'

'Right, hop in. I'm going there myself.' She hesitated and he leaned across and opened the door. 'Come on dozy, get in. Do you want me to catch it from a traffic warden for stopping at a bus stop?'

She heaved her case into the back seat and got in and almost before she could catch her breath they were on their way.

She studied his profile and the clothes he was wearing—a tweed jacket, open-necked shirt and light trousers. Obviously he was off on holiday or for the weekend. He caught her looking at him out of the corner of her eye and turned to grin at her.

'Sorry I missed the party last night—have a good time?'

'Super!' Katy lied. 'Were you supposed to

be there then?'

'Yes—I flattered myself that it was you who had invited me. At the last minute there was an emergency in the theatre. Still, I'm glad you had a good time.'

Instantly she was sorry about the lie. When the girls had decided that they would each put six names into a hat Sean's was the first one she had written. He hadn't been out with someone else after all.

'Actually I didn't enjoy it all that much,' she conceded. 'Leaving isn't the celebration for me that it is for the others. I shall be glad to begin afresh.'

'I daresay.' His eyes were on the road and he didn't mention the Underwoods or Yorkshire again.

'Are you going to visit your aunt?' Katy asked.

'Yes.' He grinned. 'A duty visit before I go off to Yorkshire for the summer. She's eighty and as deaf as a post. She also seems to be under the impression that I'm still ten years old and on my school holidays. We have chocolate cake for almost every meal!'

Katy laughed. He was quite different today—more approachable somehow. 'You'll put on weight,' she told him.

'Never mind. A few hard games of squash should put that right and she's rather an old dear really.'

As they turned into Cremorne Crescent

31

Katy wondered wistfully whether she would ever see him again. 'I shall be away for two weeks, then I have another two of my notice to work,' she told him as she reached into the back of the car for her suitcase.

He grabbed the case and hoisted it on to the pavement for her. 'Great! Maybe we'll run into each other. Have a good holiday!' And with a wave and a hoot he was gone, leaving her standing at the kerb looking after him as the yellow car roared away up the quiet road.

She let herself into the house. Dad wouldn't be home from work for over an hour yet. There would just be time for her to pop out to the shops and get his favourite pork chops for dinner—cook them just the way he liked, with orange sauce and—She stopped in the hall, sniffing as her nose picked up the unmistakable aroma of cooking. Dad must be improving if he had gone to the trouble of putting something in the oven ready for when he got home. Or maybe he had at last found an efficient daily woman. She put her case down and looked around. Yes, the place certainly did look better. There were flowers on the hall table and the furniture shone with recently applied polish.

It was a pretty house, a spacious detached, built between the wars. It had been her mother's pride and joy. She had hunted for the valued antique 'treasures' with such pleasure and had upholstered the Victorian spoon-back chairs in the living-room with her own hands. Katy went up to her old room and unpacked her case. The room was the same as it had always been, even to the row of dolls ranged along the top of the bookcase. When she came home for good she would have to redecorate it, she told herself.

From the window she could look down into the garden—the one thing her father hadn't neglected since his widowhood. It was ablaze with spring flowers and even as she stood there at the window their scent drifted up to her—wallflowers, heady and sweet, lilies-of-the-valley and the lemony fragrance of the laburnum under the window, its boughs bent under their weight of bright yellow blooms. She closed her eyes and breathed it in deeply, a wave of nostalgia washing over her. Suddenly and unaccountably her thoughts were with Sean. How on earth could she ever have imagined that he could be remotely interested in a girl like her? With the choice he had at St Anne's it was a miracle he had even noticed her. She sighed. He must have picked her for the job in Yorkshire for that very reason. She was hardly in demand—who would miss her?

Suddenly a door slammed somewhere downstairs, jerking her out of her reverie. A voice called, startling her.

'Coo-ee! Are you there? Can I come up?'

33

The voice was unfamiliar to her and she went out on to the landing and stood at the head of the stairs. At the bottom stood a woman. She was, Katy guessed, in her early thirties and very attractive with curling blonde hair and a girlishly slim figure. She was wearing a pretty summer dress in a soft blue material and she was holding a bunch of mixed flowers which she now held out to Katy.

'I've brought you some flowers. You must be Katy. I'm Isobel Johns from across the road at number five. I'm sure your father will have told you all about me.'

Katy shook her head. 'No, he didn't—' She frowned, remembering. 'Oh, he did say something about a new friend.'

The woman smiled. 'Isn't that just like David to be so vague? May I come up, dear? I'm getting a crick in my neck looking up at you like this.'

Katy began to come down. 'I'm sorry. How rude of me. It's all right. I was just coming down anyway. What can I do for you, Mrs Johns? Did you want to borrow something?'

The woman looked slightly put out. 'Borrow something? No, indeed I don't! I've come to bring you some flowers—because I know David doesn't like his garden tampered with—to introduce myself and to tell you about the casserole. All it needs is thickening and the potatoes are in the saucepan ready to

34

pop on.'

Katy blushed. 'Oh—so it was you. I'm terribly sorry. I didn't know.'

'Well, you wouldn't if your father hasn't told you about me. I expect he thought it would be better to wait till you came home.' She slipped an arm around Katy's shoulders as they walked together towards the kitchen. 'Now, shall we have a nice cup of tea? As your father's fiancée I think we should start getting to know one another as soon as possible, don't you?'

Katy stared at her, hardly able to believe her ears. 'His *what*?' she asked incredulously.

Isobel smiled serenely as she bustled about the kitchen, putting the flowers in water and filling the kettle. It was all too clear that she was perfectly at home there. 'I believe in being direct,' she said frankly. 'You have to know sometime and the sooner the better if you ask me. David has a terrible habit of putting things off. I told him you had a right to know from the beginning and when we finally made up our minds he promised me he'd write and let you know.' She shook her head. 'I guessed he'd leave it till he saw you.'

Katy sat down at the kitchen table, her knees suddenly weak. She felt as though all the breath had been knocked from her body. Dad—getting engaged—to this woman. It was true that she was attractive and obviously efficient as a housewife too—but she was years younger. There was something faintly indecent about it.

'Have you lived here long?' she asked, finding her voice at last. She seemed to remember that the last time she had been home number five had been occupied by the Livseys, an elderly couple.

Isobel gave a tinkling laugh as her flower arrangement received its final tweak. 'Heavens no! I moved in just after Christmas. My husband died in a car accident ten years ago. We'd only been married two years.' She sighed and sat down opposite Katy, looking at her with large soulful blue eyes. 'I thought then that my life was over and I clung to all the threads—the flat where we'd lived, all the familiar places and things. Then one day I took a look at myself and I realised that life was passing me by. There I was just sitting there and letting it go. Time to make a completely new start, I told myself. So I packed up—sold everything, gave up my job and moved here to take the flat over the road with the Livseys. And what do you know?' Her blue eyes danced with happiness. 'Who should I meet on the very day I moved in but David! Well, it was love at first sight. It must have been fate that brought me here.'

Katy gazed at her rapturous expression and wondered sourly whether it was her father Isobel had fallen in love with or the beautiful home he owned. Suddenly something else struck her—if Dad were getting a new wife he wouldn't need her to look after him. Not only that but he wouldn't want her hanging around playing gooseberry either—and she had already given in her notice at St Anne's!

'I do wish Dad had told me about all this before,' she said glumly. 'I was coming home to look after him. I was going to tell him tonight. It was to have been a surprise. I thought he was lonely, you see.'

Isobel's tinkling laugh rang out again, grating on Katy's nerves like a steel rasp on glass. 'Lonely! Not any more!' She patted Katy's hand. 'Ah, but what a sweet, unselfish thought. I know David would never allow you to give up your nursing career on his account and you can't tell me that you don't have a full social life—plenty of boyfriends, eh?' She giggled coyly. 'I saw the gorgeous hunk of man who dropped you off outside— the one with the dashing sports car. Tell me, is he a doctor at your hospital?'

'Yes—a paediatrician,' Katy said. 'But he isn't—'

'In no time at all you'll be married yourself,' Isobel rushed on. 'And now you won't have to worry about what your poor old Daddy is doing, will you? It's the original fairy-tale ending, isn't it?'

Katy just sat there, letting the avalanche of words engulf her. She wanted to shout: 'Yes, but I've failed my finals and given in my notice! I've got nowhere to go and now you're taking my home and my father away from me too!' Instead she smiled helplessly as Isobel got to her feet and took a final look round.

'Well, I'm off. You and your father must have the first night of your visit to yourselves. It was my suggestion,' she added quickly. 'You'll have a lot to talk about.' She smiled archly. 'Maybe you've even got some exciting news for your father too,' she suggested with a wink. 'Enjoy your dinner. You'll find an apple pie and some cream in the fridge for pudding. See you tomorrow—cheeribye!'

Katy sat still at the table after she had gone, staring at the wall. She couldn't believe it. Dad—quiet Dad, and that woman with her constant chatter and her grating breeziness. He had always loved the contemplative life. What could he possibly see in her? She'd drive him mad in six months! The kitchen clock caught her eye and she got up to light the gas under the potatoes and check the casserole. It looked and smelt delicious. Well, that at least was something. She could certainly cook and the house looked like a new pin, just the way her mother had always kept it. Give Isobel her due, she obviously knew how to worm her way into a man's life.

She was dishing up when she heard her father's key in the lock and she slipped the two plates back into the oven and went into the hall to meet him. He was hanging up his

38

raincoat on the hall stand and immediately she noticed that he looked ten years younger. His hair was neatly trimmed, his shirt was crisp and spotless and you could have sliced bread with the crease in his trousers.

'Dad!' She threw her arms around him. 'It's lovely to see you.'

He hugged her, then held her at arms' length. 'Now then, let me have a look at my girl. Mmm—too thin by half. What have you been doing to yourself? All that studying—burning the midnight oil, eh?'

She kissed him. 'Well anyway *you're* looking great, Dad. Never better! Come and eat. It's all ready. I'll have it on the table by the time you've washed your hands.'

She studied him as he sat down opposite her. There was a new light in his eyes and his skin seemed to have taken on a youthful glow. *Could* he have fallen in love again? Did it really happen to people of his age? Feeling her eyes on him he looked up with a smile.

'This is delicious. I see you haven't lost your touch in spite of all the junk food you young girls seem to live on.'

'I didn't cook this, Dad,' she told him gravely. 'It was Isobel. I've met her, by the way. She came over this afternoon, soon after I arrived. She—er—told me your news.'

He laid down his knife and fork, looking slightly uncomfortable. 'Ah—well, I thought she might do that.'

39

'Did you *hope* she would, Dad?' Katy asked. 'So that you wouldn't have to tell me yourself?' She shook her head. 'It really was too bad of you, you know. Why didn't you give me some idea of what was going on before. It was quite a shock.'

'You had your exams to think about,' he hedged, not looking at her. 'And I suppose, if I'm truthful, I was just a little afraid of what you might think.' He glanced up at her shyly. 'I expect you think your Dad has gone daft in his old age!'

She laughed affectionately, all her resentment melting at the look on his face. 'Old age! Don't be so ridiculous!' She reached across the table to squeeze his hand. 'As long as you're happy, Dad—that's all that matters to me.'

'I am, Katy,' he assured her. 'And I know that you and Isobel are going to be the greatest of friends. That's a very important part of it as far as I'm concerned.'

Katy forced herself to swallow some of her earlier misgivings, but she couldn't help feeling bleak as she thought of her own future. 'Dad—' she ventured. 'Dad, I've got some bad news, I'm afraid. I failed my finals.'

His eyes clouded as they looked into hers. 'Oh, Katy, what a pity. I'm so sorry, love. Still, you can take them again in a few months, can't you? You're sure to pass next time. I expect it was a case of nerves.'

She got up to clear the table. Somehow she couldn't bring herself to tell him that she had given in her notice—that indeed she had decided to give up nursing and come home to stay. She glanced across to where he stood looking out at the garden.

'It's going to be a good year for the roses,' he observed. 'Isobel and I plan to marry in September. I hope you'll be able to come home for the wedding.'

'Oh—but of course I will—just try and stop me,' she said in an over-bright voice.

'I didn't think you'd find the time to come home after the exams,' he said as he lit his pipe. 'It'll be good to have you here for a whole weekend.'

Katy stared at his back. She was sure she had told him she was staying for two weeks when she had telephoned. If only he would listen.

'I said a fortnight,' she muttered.

He smiled as he put away his matches. 'Four nights, eh? That's even better.'

She opened her mouth to correct him, then closed it. Maybe it was better this way. There seemed little point in staying longer now. It seemed that neither Dad nor the house needed her attention any longer.

They washed up together as they had always done, then Dad announced that there was a gardening programme on TV that he wanted to watch and they settled down. It was halfway through when Katy heard the back door open and close, a moment later Isobel's head came round the living-room door.

'Just thought I'd see if everything was all right,' she mouthed at Katy.

'Fine, thanks.' With a glance at her father Katy got up and went into the hall, closing the door behind her. 'Dad drinks in every word of that TV gardener,' she explained. 'Better not interrupt.'

Isobel nodded and took her hand. 'Come upstairs with me a moment. I'd appreciate your advice.' On the landing she opened the door of Katy's room. 'I hope you won't mind, dear, but I plan to redecorate this room for David and I—for after we're married.'

'My room? But why?' Katy asked.

'Well—I wouldn't feel quite happy in the other one. I'm sure you understand. In future that can be yours when you come to stay.' She glanced at Katy. 'But I don't suppose that will be very often, will it—what with all your friends and your career? A couple of middle-aged fogies like David and I will bore you to death, I'm sure.' She walked round the room, her eyes half-closed. 'I thought a nice lilac,' she mused, 'with maybe a moss green carpet—and a new suite of course. Or perhaps some built-in fitments. Do you want to keep all those old dolls, dear? Or shall I arrange to get rid of them for you?'

42

'I'll keep them, thanks,' Katy said stiffly. 'Maybe you won't mind if I leave them in the box-room—or will that inconvenience you?' she added meaningly.

Isobel looked at her. 'No—as long as it isn't for too long.' She bit her lip. 'Just between ourselves I have hopes that we may be needing the box-room for a nursery. I always wanted a family and if we don't waste too much time it could still happen, couldn't it?'

Katy's stomach turned over. 'I—I think I'll go and make some coffee,' she muttered.

Afterwards she couldn't imagine how she got through the evening. In spite of what she'd said about them having their first evening alone together Isobel stayed on, chattering animatedly all through the television programmes. Just before she left she looked at Katy and said:

'Have you told your father yet about the boyfriend?'

David Lang took his pipe out of his mouth and looked up with interest. 'What's this? I haven't heard anything about a boyfriend.'

Before Katy had time to reply Isobel rushed on. 'A handsome doctor from the hospital with the raciest little car you ever saw! Caused quite a stir in the road, I can tell you. What did you say his name was, dear?'

'I didn't—but it's Sean MacInnon.' Katy was about to add that it was all a mistake and that he wasn't her boyfriend when she suddenly had an idea. Sean might make a useful excuse if things became too unbearable here.

'How long have you been going out together?' her father asked.

She shrugged. 'Oh—some time.'

'And is it—serious?'

Katy blushed and Isobel laughed shrilly. 'David! Don't embarrass the girl. One look was enough to see that the man obviously adores her! And any girl would be mad to let a man like him slip through her fingers!' She perched girlishly on the arm of David's chair and slipped her arm possessively round his neck. 'Believe me, *I* know a good man when I see one, don't I, darling?'

Katy groaned inwardly. She *was* going to need that excuse, there was no doubt about it—and probably sooner than she had thought!

## CHAPTER FOUR

Katy had never been more glad to be back at work than she was on that Monday morning two weeks later. Two days had been more than enough of being at home. Isobel was hardly ever out of the house and her father was obviously besotted. She felt totally in the

44

way. On Sunday afternoon when the telephone had rung and Katy had answered it to find a caller ringing the wrong number she had seized her opportunity.

'Sean darling!' she shouted into the bewildered caller's ear with a flash of inspiration. 'Well—I don't know. I did promise to stay on here another couple of days but if you really want me to go with you. All right then, darling—see you later. I'm sure Dad will understand. Bye.' She had carried on her one-sided conversation loud enough for her father and Isobel in the other room to hear and when she rejoined them they were looking at each other knowingly.

'Don't tell me—there's some party or other on and your boyfriend wants you to go with him,' her father said.

'Oh Dad, I hope you don't mind—' She couldn't help noticing Isobel's look of relief. 'Sean says he misses me and—well, you know how it is.'

He had insisted on driving her to the bus station and of course Isobel had come too, kissing her fondly as she got on to the bus and making her promise to 'bring that young man home soon so that we can get a good look at him'.

As she waved them goodbye she swallowed the lump in her throat, wishing that all the lies she had told could have been true. The rest of her two weeks' holiday stretched

45

before her like a yawning cavern—boring and empty. When she arrived back at the flat Tracy and Sonia told her that they had given the landlord notice. Secretly she thought they might have consulted her first, but there wasn't much point. She couldn't have afforded to stay on alone anyway.

By the time she went back to work she was almost desperate. Where was she to go—and what was she to do? Everyone was so full of their own plans that they didn't seem to have time to listen to her problems. She had lain awake night after night, thinking about them and now, as far as she could see, there was only one course left open to her. Much as she hated the idea she would have to pocket her pride and ask Sean MacInnon if his offer was still open. The idea of approaching him terrified her—but the idea that the job might have been filled terrified her even more!

When she reported for duty that morning she found that many of the girls she was working with were from the new intake but that the newly-appointed Staff Nurse was from her own year. Karen Grainger had never been a friend of hers and now she found herself treated in the same way as the new student nurses. Katy hated it. Thank goodness it was only for another two weeks, she told herself. When it was time for the doctor's round she looked anxiously for Sean and when she caught sight of his dark head in the ward doorway her heart skipped a beat.

'Nurse Lang, have you got the notes for the new admission?' Karen Grainger snapped. 'Mr MacInnon is here to see him.'

Katy glared at Karen and fetched the notes, hurrying over to the bedside of a small boy who had been brought in the night before. She handed them to Sean, noting with dismay his curt nod to her. She might have been a student nurse to him too. He examined the child carefully, reading the GP's notes, then he straightened and looked at her.

'Peter came in last night with a severe asthma attack,' he told her. 'I want him monitored with a peak-flow meter. You're familiar with the procedure, aren't you?'

'Yes.' She followed him down the ward.

Suddenly he turned to her. 'How would you diagnose asthma in that child?' he asked her.

Surprised she glanced round at the little boy in the bed. 'Well—there is a rounding of the shoulders and the chest is slightly distended,' she said.

He nodded. 'And if you were to listen to his chest what would you expect to hear?'

'Wheezing.'

'Because—?'

'Because the airways are irritated.'

'Right. Give me the three most likely causes.'

'Allergy, infection and emotion,' she said without hesitation.

'And can you tell me the one important difference between asthma and other chest diseases.'

She considered, wrinkling her brow in concentration. 'In asthma the shortness of breath becomes progressively worse after exercise, whilst in other diseases of the chest it improves immediately with rest.'

He nodded, apparently satisfied. 'Well done, Nurse Lang. I would like you to take special care of Peter whilst he's here,' he said. 'He's rather a timid little boy and it's important that he feels at ease while he's undergoing tests. It's clear that he's taken to you. I'll have a word with Sister.' He was turning to leave the ward and she caught at his sleeve. It was now or never.

'Please—can I talk to you?' she asked, her heart beating fast.

He looked down at her. 'Of course you can.'

She glanced round. 'Not here—I—could I see you later?' Her cheeks were scarlet.

'In the canteen at lunch time—twelve-thirty,' he said abruptly.

When he had gone Karen Grainger came up to her. 'You really mustn't try to engage the doctors in conversation, Nurse,' she said loftily. 'Don't you realise that their time is precious?'

Katy looked at her, her temper flaring. 'Mind your own business!' she snapped. 'And get lost!'

Karen peered at her indignantly from behind her spectacles. 'Really, Nurse Lang! I shall have to report you to Sister if you speak to me like that again.'

'Be my guest!' Katy invited. 'But you'd better hurry up or you'll lose your chance. I'm leaving the week after next!' As she turned triumphantly away she caught sight of Peter's face and winked wickedly at him.

As soon as she had finished her chores she went back to his bedside. He was an engaging little chap with bright ginger hair and freckles. While she worked his eyes had followed her round the ward and now that she had time to give him her attention he was obviously delighted. She picked up the colouring book he was looking at.

'This is nice. Don't you want to colour some of the pictures?' she asked him.

He shook his head. 'I haven't got any crayons.'

'Oh dear, that won't do. I'll see if I can find some for you if you like. Or, better still, you could go into the playroom and find them for yourself. You might even find another little boy to play with in there.'

His smile vanished and he hung his head. 'I can't,' he mumbled. 'Playing makes me cough and I can't breathe—like last night.'

She patted his shoulder. 'Never mind. We'll find out why that is and see if we can make you better, shall we? In the meantime I shall have to try and find the time to come and play with you myself shan't I?'

The grin returned and she noticed that his two front teeth were missing leaving an endearing gap.

'I like you,' he confided. 'What's your name?'

'I'm Nurse Lang, but you can call me Katy if you like—as long as you don't let Sister or Staff hear you, right? It'll be our secret, eh?'

He nodded conspiratorially. 'You're the only person I know who's got hair the same colour as mine,' he told her. 'Do they call you "Carrots" too?'

She shook her head, frowning fiercely. 'They wouldn't dare! Actually, Peter, when you're grown up people seem to like it better. They stop calling you all those rude things.' At the back of her mind she was remembering Sean calling her 'Marigold'— well, it was an improvement on 'Carrots'.

She was late for her lunch break. It was nothing unusual on the children's ward, they were notoriously difficult with their meals. When she finally did arrive at the canteen she quite expected Sean to have gone, and at first she thought he had as she stood on tiptoe to scan the sea of heads. Then she saw him on the far side of the room. He was drinking a cup of coffee and he had even tipped up the chair opposite—saving it for her? She hurried across to him.

'Sorry I'm late.'

He glanced up at her. 'Your cap is crooked.'

She pulled it off and succeeded in loosening most of her hair at the same time. He looked amused.

'Aren't you eating?'

She lifted her shoulders, frantically trying to tuck her hair back into its chignon. 'I was afraid you might have given up and gone. I wanted to talk to you,' she said through a mouthful of pins. 'It doesn't matter about lunch.'

'Don't be so stupid!' he admonished. 'How can you expect to care for your patients if you neglect yourself? It's one of the first basics of nursing.' He glared at her. 'What happens if you don't eat?'

She bit her lip. 'The blood sugar level is lowered,' she answered meekly.

'And what effect does that have?'

'It—it slows up the reactions.' Her temper was rising again. Why was he behaving like a Dickensian schoolmaster this morning? And why was she letting him get away with it? 'Well—that's the answer you were looking for isn't it?' she demanded. 'You seem to have forgotten that I'm giving up nursing. You can forget the lectures now, you know!' Her eyes

51

flashed at him dangerously but his own dark ones glared back relentlessly.

'While you're looking after my patients you're still a nurse as far as I am concerned and you *will* have something to eat—and as many lectures as I think you need—Nurse Lang.' He got to his feet. 'I can recommend the egg, sausage and chips—and I don't want to hear that it's fattening! Tea or coffee?'

She sniffed. 'Coffee.'

She watched as he went across to the counter. What was the matter with everyone today? If only he could have been in the mood he had shown her when he gave her a lift home. What she had to ask him would be doubly difficult now.

As she tucked into the sausage, egg and chips she realised for the first time how hungry she was. He watched her in silence for a while, then asked:

'Well, what was it you wanted to speak to me about?'

She swallowed, then looked at him, one eyebrow raised perversely. 'Don't you know that it's very bad for the digestion to talk and eat at the same time?'

He began to get up. 'I've more to do with my time than sit here listening to your impertinence!'

Panic rose in her throat, almost choking her. 'Oh, please—I didn't mean to be rude. Don't go!' Several people looked round in amusement at her crimson-faced confusion and Sean looked more annoyed than ever. She took a deep breath. 'Look—I do have something to say—something important—and—and difficult.'

He sat down again, his face as dark as thunder. 'Well for heaven's sake say it before you have half the hospital gossiping about us!'

She laid down her knife and fork. 'That job you told me about—in Yorkshire. Have you filled it yet?'

He looked at her for a long moment. 'Are you trying to tell me that you've changed your mind?' he asked.

She shrugged. 'I might have.'

He stood up. 'Well, I'll give you until this evening to make up your mind about it,' he told her tersely. 'I'll be at your flat this evening at eight. If you've managed to decide what you want to do we'll talk about it then.' And without another word or a backward glance he was gone.

Katy knew she would have the flat to herself when she got home that evening. Tracy had gone up North for an interview and Sonia had a date with a new boyfriend. She showered and changed though Sean hadn't said he was taking her out. Maybe he would only stay long enough to tell her the details about the job. After some consideration she put on her new stretch jeans and a fluffy cream sweater, tying up her

53

unruly hair in a ponytail.

He was prompt, ringing the doorbell dead on eight o'clock. She had found half a bottle of sherry at the back of the kitchen cupboard, left over from the party, and had put it out on the sideboard with two glasses so that she could offer him a drink. He accepted.

'Thanks, I will. It's been quite a day one way and another. Tell me, how have you got along with Peter?'

She smiled as she poured two glasses of sherry and handed one to him. 'Fine. He's a super little boy. It's a pity he's so hung up about playing with the other children though.'

He nodded. 'I've been looking through the notes his GP sent through, I also rang him this afternoon for a chat. It seems Peter's parents are divorced and he and his mother live with the grandmother so that she can care for Peter while his mother goes to work. His asthma is almost certainly allergic. He didn't have it until he went to live with his grandmother and she is a cat person—she breeds Siamese, it seems the house is full of them. But she is convinced that his trouble is emotional—caused by the divorce. She coddles him, thinks of him as "delicate"— instills into him that he will be ill if he runs and plays with the other kids.' He spread his hands. 'You've seen the result.'

She shook her head. 'What can be done

54

about it?'

'Ideally he and his mother should move to a place of their own, away from the cats and the grandmother's influence. But it isn't as easy as that. Peter's mother needs the money she earns, she couldn't afford to pay someone to look after Peter during the day.'

'Now that he's started school couldn't she find a job that would fit in with his hours?'

He pulled a face. 'You know how hard jobs are to find. That's something for the hospital social worker to sort out. Our job is to convince her—the mother, that is—that Peter's trouble is being caused essentially by the cats. It isn't always easy to accept a fact that is going to make life difficult for us, is it?'

She digested this last remark, knowing all too well how true it was.

Sean leaned forward. 'Katy—don't tell me that you're not cut out to be a nurse. It just isn't true and you know it, don't you? You're not going to let one setback ruin a good career, are you?'

She refused to look at him, twisting her fingers in her lap. 'I've given in my notice now,' she said in a small voice. 'I can't take it back—I won't.'

'All right. But look, if you take this temporary job for the summer I can put in a word for you if you like. You could start again in the autumn. You'd miss the next sitting but you could take your finals again in the winter. What do you say?'

'I'll take the job if it's still on offer,' she said noncommitally.

He smiled. 'I always knew you would in the end. I think you just wanted me to twist your arm a little, didn't you, Katy?'

She looked up at him, her eyes blazing. 'Don't be so damned arrogant! If you really want to know, the only reason I'm accepting the job is that I've no choice. I've no job and—and no home either!' Then, to her utter horror, her throat tightened and tears began to roll helplessly down her cheeks. Sean stared at her in alarm.

'What on earth do you mean—no home? Has something happened to your father?'

She nodded, gulping speechlessly.

'Good Lord! I'm terribly sorry, Katy. When did this happen?'

'When I went home a month ago.' She swallowed hard, dabbing at her face with the sleeve of her sweater. 'There was this woman who announced that she was his fiancée. It was awful. They didn't want me at all. She made it clear that she doesn't expect me to be around much after they're married either. And there was I thinking that he needed me—stupidly giving up my job to go and be with him,' she ended bitterly, her voice catching.

She had expected him to have a good laugh

but he didn't. Instead he moved across to sit next to her on the settee, handing her his large handkerchief.

'Here—you'll shrink that sleeve. Why is it that girls never seem to have handkerchieves?' He touched her arm. 'Katy—I hate to say I told you so, but I always thought you were making a mistake running home to your father. If you're really honest with yourself that is what you were doing, isn't it—running away?'

She shook her head angrily, the tears flowing even faster. 'It isn't true! How dare you say it is!'

He slipped an arm round her. 'Go on, admit it—you'll feel better once you've faced up to the fact. Home was a nice safe little bolt-hole where you could hide and lick your wounds. But your father is still a comparatively young man. You should be glad that he's found someone he can be happy with again. I'm sure you will be once the shock has worn off.'

'You don't understand,' she protested. 'She's *years* younger than he is—she's—she's even talking about having babies!'

'Oh, I see—you're afraid you won't be Daddy's little girl any longer—is that it?'

She pulled away from him, moving to the other end of the settee. 'That's a rotten thing to say. You don't know what you're talking about—how can you? That woman never owned a home of her own and now she wants my mother's. She's going to change everything to suit her own tastes. She's even taking over my room for them to share after they're married. She's kicking me out—and Dad is just letting her.'

'Maybe he thinks you should have your independence,' Sean said gently. 'It's what most girls want—don't you, Katy?'

'I don't seem to be getting much choice in the matter, do I?' she said miserably.

He sighed, shaking his head. 'The modern woman never ceases to amaze me. One minute it's all women's lib—the next you're weeping because some man doesn't need you to cook and clean and give up everything for him! I'll never understand.'

She sniffed, trying desperately to control the tears. 'Nobody asked you to,' she said perversely.

He stood up, pulling her to her feet and lifting her chin with one finger. 'Now—what is it to be—do I ring the Underwoods and tell them I've found someone for them?'

She nodded.

'But do you really want the job, Katy? I mean, I wouldn't like to think it was *only* a stop-gap for you. We must consider the child.'

'Of course I want it,' she said crossly. 'Do you think I'd have demeaned myself in front of you if I hadn't wanted it?'

He smiled. 'I told you I had a feeling you'd be back asking for it, didn't I? I've always been lucky when it comes to getting my own way, Katy.'

A sharp retort rose to her lips but before it could pass them she found them otherwise occupied as Sean bent his head to kiss her swiftly.

'I'm travelling up to Belldale on the eighth,' he told her tugging her hair teasingly. 'Be ready at about eight. I'll pick you up.'

'No thank you. I prefer to go by train,' she said, breathlessly disentangling herself from his arms. 'If you'll just give me the address.'

He didn't argue but took a card from his pocket and wrote quickly on it. 'The nearest railway station is eight miles away. A taxi will cost you a fortune so you'd better ring when you arrive and one of us will come and collect you.' He looked at her quizzically. 'Or would you rather walk?'

'I'll manage,' she said crossly. Right at that moment she was hating herself. Why had she let him see her cry—allowed him to see how vulnerable she was? Now that he knew her weak spot he would think he could do as he liked with her. Play with her emotions for his own amusement. Now, more than ever, it was necessary to show him that she could be strong.

'Please don't get any wrong ideas about me,' she said shakily. 'I know you think that you have only to crook your little finger and a girl like me will fall down in a dead faint at the honour you've done her. But you may not always be right!' She stared at him, her cheeks very pink. 'If you think that all you have to do is kiss me—' she broke off, biting her lip. 'What I'm trying to say is that I'll come to Yorkshire on the strict understanding that our relationship is purely professional!' she finished on an inspired note.

He shrugged his shoulders lazily. 'Well, of course—if that's what you really want, Katy. Goodnight.'

She closed the door behind him with a hollow feeling inside her. What had possessed her to say a thing like that? What demon of stupid pride was it that was always making her say things she didn't mean?

## CHAPTER FIVE

The last few days at the flat were hectic. Tracy was leaving to take the job she had been offered in Newcastle while Sonia was staying on at St Anne's to take her midwifery course—she was moving out to share a flat with one of the social workers. The place was chaotic, with suitcases and half-filled boxes everywhere and, Katy reflected as she stared about her at the mass of clothes and possessions strewn around the room, it was amazing what one could accumulate in just three short years. She could hardly cart this lot up to Yorkshire with her, yet Isobel would not be pleased to see her turning up with a mass of stuff to be stored at home. In the end she packed only her newest things and stuffed everything else into a bag to take to the local charity shop, saving only Arnold the battered teddy bear who had sat on her pillow ever since she could remember.

The night before they left the girls gave the inevitable party, but Katy wasn't in the mood for celebrating so decided to take herself off to the cinema. The future seemed so uncertain and insecure. For the first time in her life she didn't really know where she was going, and she didn't like the feeling at all. On her way she called in at the railway station to enquire about the trains up to Yorkshire, thinking that she might as well save time by buying her ticket too. The man in the ticket office stared at her in startled disbelief.

'Blimey! Don't you ever read the papers or look at the telly?' he asked.

Katy shook her head. 'I haven't lately—why?'

'You can't have!' He laughed. 'If you had you'd know about the rail strike.'

'Strike? You mean there are no trains?' she asked plaintively.

'Not after midnight tonight,' he told her

triumphantly.

Her heart sank. 'Oh—when will it be over?'

'Better ask the Government, love,' came the reply as he turned away.

Katy walked slowly out on to the street again. Now what was she going to do? Her interest for the film she had been about to see evaporated and she turned her footsteps back in the direction of the flat. It was just possible that someone else would be travelling North tomorrow. But the party was in full swing and she found it impossible to make herself heard above the din of the record player. Finally, there was only one person she could think of.

Standing in the hall and blocking up one ear as firmly as she could she dialled her father's number. To her relief he answered quickly.

'Katy, love!' He sounded surprised. 'I'm so glad you rang. Isn't it tomorrow you go off up to this new job you wrote about?'

'Yes—Dad, I can't hear you very well, there's a party going on here. Can I come home tonight? Do you mind?'

'Mind? Of course not. Love to have you, even if it is only for one night. By the way, how are you getting there tomorrow?'

'Well, that's just it, Dad. I didn't know about this strike until just now. Actually I'm a bit stuck.'

'Mmm—well, don't worry. Maybe I can drive you up there. Come home and we'll talk about it.'

She felt much better as she replaced the receiver and, elbowing her way through the crowd, she collected her suitcases and quietly left, hastily scribbling a note for the girls and pinning it on the kitchen bulletin board.

When she arrived at Cremorne Crescent her father opened the door to her, looking harassed.

'Isobel has just been over,' he told her as he filled the kettle. 'She reminded me that I was taking her to the coast tomorrow for a picnic.' He shook his head. 'My memory gets worse!'

Katy's heart sank. 'I don't want to spoil your plans, Dad,' she assured him. 'You mustn't disappoint Isobel.' She peered at him. 'I hope you didn't fall out over it.'

'No—no.' He poured the boiling water onto the tea and looked up at her with a smile. 'She has far too sweet a nature for that. Actually, she said she would think of a plan to get you there. She's gone home to think it all out.' He patted her shoulder. 'She's a real gem you know.'

Katy frowned. 'Maybe I should make some other enquiries myself.'

He shook his head firmly. 'Just relax and leave it all to Isobel. She won't let you down. She's a wizard when it comes to organising.' He smiled dreamily. 'You know, sometimes I

63

wonder how I ever got along without her.'

Katy took her father's advice and relaxed. Once she had stretched out on the settee in the living-room with a cup of her father's good strong tea in her hand, she realised for the first time how hectic the past week had been and how tired she was. The last days at the hospital had been exhausting both physically and mentally and she had come under fire from Sister Blake and the Senior Nursing Officer. They had both insisted that she was making a sad mistake in giving up her nursing and should be staying on to take her finals again as soon as possible. But Sister Blake had at least agreed that the temporary job in Yorkshire would give her time to sort out her feelings and decide what she really wanted. Now she was glad to be away from the pressures at last.

For once Isobel did not put in an appearance and she and her father chatted until late. It was just like it had been in the old days and as the evening went by she grew more relaxed until at last her eyelids began to droop and she felt hazy.

'Katy, love—better get up to bed. You've a journey in front of you in the morning, don't forget.' Her father gently shook her shoulder.

Katy nodded and heaved herself up from the settee. 'Yes, you're right, Dad.' She kissed the top of his head. 'Thanks for a lovely evening. Goodnight.'

It seemed as though she had been asleep for only a few minutes when she was awakened by a tap on the door and Dad coming in with a cup of tea.

'Seven o'clock, love. Time you were thinking about getting up.'

She smiled sleepily. 'You're spoiling me.'

He grinned ruefully. 'Well and why not? I shan't get many more chances, shall I?'

She heard Isobel's voice downstairs while she was in the bath and when she opened the kitchen door she was greeted by the sight of her prospective stepmother in a frilly apron, cooking breakfast.

'Good morning, Katy darling,' she said with the brightest of smiles. 'I wanted to make sure you had a proper breakfast inside you before making a long trip like this. Oh, and by the way, your chauffeur will be here at about nine.'

Katy sat down at the table, laid with a crisp checked cloth, and looked at the plate loaded with bacon, eggs and fried bread that Isobel placed before her. 'Chauffeur—who would that be?'

'Ah—wait and see.' Isobel looked smug. 'You know, Katy, you don't always win by being a liberated woman. Sometimes it pays to pretend to be just a tiny bit helpless.' She giggled. 'I believe women should liberate themselves by using the assets God gave them.'

Katy smiled politely. Isobel might have been speaking in Chinese for all she understood her. She did justice to the bacon and eggs then went upstairs to collect her things together, wondering who Isobel had managed to find to give her a lift. It was while she was taking a last look in the mirror that she heard a car draw up outside and Isobel's voice gushing as she opened the front door. As she reached the top of the stairs she heard her father's voice join in, then suddenly she caught something that Isobel was saying and froze in her tracks.

'We've been hoping *so* much to get the chance of meeting you. Of course Katy has told us *all* about you. I think it's so *romantic*, the two of you on a sort of mission to help this poor little boy. You'll learn a lot about each other in the weeks to come, you know—and that's important. One can be so impetuous when one is young and in love.'

'Oh, you're so *right*, Mrs Johns!' Sean took a step into the hall and looked straight up at Katy where she stood on the stairs, her face crimson. 'Ah, there you are—darling!' His eyes twinkled wickedly. 'What a silly goose you are! Why didn't you tell me you were having difficulties in getting to Yorkshire?'

Three pairs of eyes were on her and Katy knew a moment of blind panic when it was all she could do not to turn and run. She took a firm hold of herself. There was nothing for it

66

but to brazen it out.

'I've been so busy that I didn't hear about the rail strike until last night,' she said. 'I—I thought you'd already gone.'

Isobel gave her tinkling laugh. 'Really! Fancy not knowing each other's travelling arrangements. Anyone would think you two had been having a lovers' tiff. Now you can have a nice cosy drive together, can't you?' She seized Katy and kissed her soundly. Just for a moment it looked as though she might bestow the same treatment on Sean, but, much to Katy's relief she thought better of it, satisfying herself by saying,

'Now off you go and don't forget to write, will you?'

Dad hugged her, Sean picked up her case and a moment later she was in the car, feeling very hot and dreading the explanation she must make in the coming minutes. They were just pulling away from the kerb when there was a shrill cry from Isobel who came running after them, waving something yellow. She caught up with the slowing car and dropped something into Katy's lap through the window. It was Arnold the battered teddy bear.

'Mustn't go without this old chap,' she puffed. 'I know how you feel about him.'

'Thanks!' Katy pushed Arnold out of sight into her zipped holdall and stole a glance at Sean's profile as he drew out into the road again. His shoulders were shaking with silent laughter.

'It's not what you're thinking,' she said grimly, without looking at him. 'And this wasn't my idea. The last thing I want is to put you to any trouble.'

'Oh but you haven't,' he said, his voice still shaking with amusement. 'I wouldn't have missed that for the world! Your face as you stood there on the stairs was an absolute *study*!' He gave a shout of laughter. 'I can't think what you can have told them about me.'

Katy winced, her cheeks burning and her hands clenched into fists in her lap. 'I told you,' she said with exaggerated patience. 'It was all a misunderstanding—well almost. The last time I went home—when I found out about Dad's engagement—I needed an excuse to get away. Isobel had seen me getting out of your car that day and she assumed that we were—' She glanced at him uncomfortably. 'She's a lady who jumps to conclusions.'

'And you did nothing to disillusion her,' he said smiling smugly.

'I didn't get the *chance*,' she protested. 'You don't know Isobel—she isn't really interested in what other people have to say. She likes her own version best! Anyway, one day when the phone rang and it was someone with a wrong number I pretended it was you—asking me to go back.' She glared at him, hating him for his obvious enjoyment of her discomfort. 'Anyway, there you are. I owed you an explanation and that's it, for what it's worth!'

He raised an eyebrow at her. 'And do I hear "Thank you very much for coming to my rescue, Sean"? Surely you're not too embarrassed to show a little appreciation?'

'I'm only human,' she said miserably. 'You can hardly expect me to thank you for giving me the most embarrassing moment of my life! If you want to drop me off now that you've had a good laugh I can always hitch-hike up to Yorkshire.'

He frowned. 'Don't be so childish. Why don't you try laughing for a change?'

'With all that's happened lately my sense of humour seems to have been rather battered.' She sniffed, dangerously close to tears. Oh God! Surely she wasn't going to top everything else by crying in front of him again! She swallowed hard and said in a small voice, 'Thank you for giving me this lift. It isn't that I'm not grateful. It was just—just the way it came about. I'm sorry.'

'Apology accepted. Now, let's forget the whole thing, shall we?' He pressed his foot down hard on the accelerator and the car leapt forward. They drove in silence for a while, then he turned to her.

'I almost forgot, I have some news for you. Peter Daniels, our little asthma patient, and his mother are moving house shortly. They

69

came to see me yesterday—oh, and by the way, Peter sends you his love.'

Katy looked up, her expression brightening. 'That's great news! He improved quite a lot during the few days he was in hospital. I even managed to get him playing with the other children before he left.'

'I know and his mother was very grateful to you for that—and for the skin tests we ran that proved Peter's allergy to her mother's cats. Through the social worker she has been able to get one of those new flats that have just been finished on the big new development on the outskirts of town—*and* a secretarial job at the school Peter will be going to. I hope it will mean an end to all his problems.'

'I hope Toby Underwood's case will be as easy to solve,' Katy said.

He shook his head. 'I'm afraid that's not very likely. Its cause could be one of so many factors. We've already investigated the possibility of allergy and infection, as you would imagine—only to find nothing. His asthma is obviously of the intrinsic kind and yet he doesn't strike one as an over-emotional child.'

Katy looked thoughtful. 'He has had a number of traumatic happenings in his young life from what you've told me. His mother dying—being sent away from home and now—' She looked at him meaningly. 'Now a

70

new stepmother.'

Sean shook his head. 'I see what you mean but you can't compare his case with yours. Claire is the best thing that ever happened to Toby. He quite clearly adores her and as for school, do you know that it has been discovered through research that a great percentage of these children benefit from removal from their parents. That's why there are special schools for asthmatic children.'

'I know. I've been reading the subject up,' she told him. 'But you can't lay down hard and fast rules with asthmatics. It has been known to work in reverse. It's a known fact that one aspect of the "asthmatic personality" if such a thing exists is to bottle up feelings. Toby might well have suffered without confiding in anyone.'

He turned to smile at her. 'You have been doing your homework, haven't you? Yes, it's a very complex subject, which is what makes it so fascinating—unless of course you happen to be the unfortunate sufferer. What I'd like you to do, Katy, is to monitor Toby very closely, but without making it too obvious. Play down the nurse part of the job and concentrate more on the "companion". I believe you're just the person to do it.'

She smiled, flushing with pleasure. 'Thank you. I'll certainly do my best.'

He glanced at his watch. 'What about lunch?'

'Let me buy yours,' she said impulsively. 'In return for the lift.'

He smiled ruefully. 'The day I let a girl pay for my lunch she'll have to owe me more than a seat in my car!'

'That's a very chauvinistic point of view,' Katy remarked.

He swung the car off the road and on to the forecourt of an attractive small pub. 'Yes, isn't it!'

The Wheatsheaf Inn was small but comfortable and served a delicious ploughman's lunch with crusty bread, cheese, pickles and a crisp salad. By the time they resumed their drive Katy felt pleasantly full, and with the warm sun on the windscreen she soon found herself nodding. Sean looked at her.

'Sleepy?'

She blinked hard. 'I had a late night. Dad and I sat up talking.'

He smiled. 'Why fight it? If you press the lever on your right the seat will recline. Why not have forty winks as my grandfather used to call it?'

When Katy opened her eyes again it was to a wide arc of clear blue sky. The car was beginning its descent of a steep hill and on all sides there was rolling moorland. She sat up and rubbed her eyes.

'Where are we?'

Sean smiled. 'Ah, so you're awake. I was

just going to stop and give you a nudge. We're almost there. At the foot of this hill is the village of Belldon Cross and Bridge House is on the outskirts.'

'And your house?' she asked.

'About another couple of miles farther on,' he told her. 'I'll drop you off first. I telephoned Claire last night after your prospective stepmama had SOS'd for help to let her know when to expect us.' He turned to look at her as she took out her handbag mirror and peered anxiously into it. 'You look perfectly all right. Don't worry.'

She tugged at her hair, which as usual was escaping in wispy tendrils. 'It would have been nice to have been able to freshen up a little first,' she muttered.

He pulled the car over to the side of the road and stopped, turning to her with a smile. 'Go on then, do whatever it is you have to. I'll wait.'

Flashing him a grateful look she pulled out a comb, compact and lipstick and repaired her make-up as best she could whilst he watched with lazy amusement.

'I liked you better the way you were before,' he observed. 'All rosy and tousled with sleep—very sexy, like a newly-opened flower.' He leaned over to touch her cheek, then bent his head to kiss her lightly on the lips. She caught her breath a little and lifted her hand to his, but he drew back, misinterpreting her action.

'Ah—sorry. I was forgetting your condition for accepting this job.'

She looked at him. 'What condition?'

'Surely you can't have forgotten it, Katy?' His eyes were enigmatic. 'Our relationship is to remain purely professional—remember?'

She looked away, biting her lip. 'Of course—but—'

He leaned towards her again, his eyes twinkling. 'Of course we could always put it down to gratitude. After all, I did come to your rescue, didn't I?'

She stiffened. He was laughing at her again. 'Isn't it time we were going?' she asked.

He shook his head. 'There's no hurry. You'll find life much more leisurely up here in Yorkshire, that's one of the nice things about it.' He smiled at her. 'What was it your future stepmother said—that we'd discover a great deal about one another? I'd like that, Katy—I'd like to know what there is under all that fierce independence. Somehow I suspect that you're really just a frightened little girl, aren't you?'

'Save the psychoanalysis for your patients!' she said hotly, acutely embarrassed by the scrutiny of his dark eyes.

He straightened his back and turned his eyes to the road again, switching on the engine and urging the car forward. He neither spoke nor glanced at her again and she sank back in her seat, swamped by dismay and disappointment. Why could she never carry off a situation like this without appearing rude and gauche? And was that really the way he saw her—'A frightened little girl'? Had his kiss merely been intended to reassure her—a boost to her confidence? Now, because of her fatally hasty tongue, she might never know.

## CHAPTER SIX

As Sean had said, the village of Belldon Cross began at the foot of the hill and spread out around the ankles of the moor like a lace frill on the hem of a petticoat. Katy watched with delight as the stark beauty of the moor gave way to blossoming hawthorn and broom, and the frothy freshness of lilac and apple trees in cottage gardens. The landscape softened as the afternoon sun turned the grey stone of the cottage walls to silver, and ahead of them she glimpsed the glimmer of water through the trees.

The road dipped on, ending at the bottom in a double bend, crowned by an old stone bridge that crossed the river. On the far bank stood a low L-shaped house, built of the same stone as the cottages in the village. It had mullioned windows and a moss-covered roof.

Before it, a garden rambled down to the riverbank while to its rear the moor rose steeply, divided by drystone walls. In the distance she could see sheep grazing on the rough, gorse-spangled grass. She looked enquiringly at Sean who nodded.

'Yes, that's it—Bridge House. Rather nice, isn't it?'

'Oh, it's beautiful!'

They crossed the little bridge where fast-flowing water bubbled over smooth stones and for a moment lost sight of the house as it disappeared behind a screen of tall trees. Then Sean nosed the car in through a pair of white gates on to a wide gravelled drive lined with rhododendron bushes. As they neared the house the bushes gave on to a small clearing of grass in the centre of which was a huge cedar tree. From the lowest branch hung a swing on which a small, dark-haired boy was sitting. As soon as he saw the car he jumped up and ran towards them, shouting and waving his arms excitedly.

'Uncle Sean! Uncle Sean!' The childish voice was shrill with delight.

Sean braked and stopped the car. 'Hello, Toby. You've grown so much I hardly recognised you! This is Katy Lang who I've brought with me to keep you out of mischief.'

Katy found herself looking into two enormous grave brown eyes. She smiled.

'Hello, Toby. I've been hearing so much about you and about this super place. I'm sure we're all going to have a lovely time.'

The dark eyes examined her face for a moment, solemn and serious, then they broke into a smile. 'Hello.' He caught at her hand. 'Would you like to come and try my swing? Mr Oldershaw who comes to do the garden made it for me yesterday. It can go ever so high.'

Katy laughed. 'I can't wait to have a go on it, Toby, but don't you think I'd better go and meet your parents first?'

He nodded thoughtfully. 'Oh—I s'pose so.' He touched the car's smooth yellow bonnet with an admiring finger. 'Is this the new car? Can it go very fast?'

'Like the wind. Hop in and you can ride up to the house with us,' Sean said. 'And maybe tomorrow I'll take you for a drive.'

Katy opened the door and made room for Toby beside her. He squeezed in, wriggling with excitement. 'A picnic! Let's go for a picnic—and exploring!' he asked breathlessly. 'Can we? *Can we?*'

Sean laughed, pressing his foot down hard on the accelerator to speed up the last stretch of the drive. 'All right, you're on—a picnic it shall be!'

As they drew up in front of the house a woman came out on to the porch to meet them. She was in her thirties, slim and dark, her hair caught back in an elegant French pleat. She wore a blue tweed skirt and a white blouse with a blue cashmere cardigan thrown casually across her shoulders. As the car braked, throwing up a shower of gravel, she laughed and came towards them.

'Sean! Will you never grow up? You're a menace to life and limb!'

'Don't be cross with him, he was showing me how fast his new car can go,' Toby defended as he scrambled out. 'And look—this is Katy Lang who's come to stay with us. Isn't she pretty?'

Katy blushed as the older woman held out her hand, laughing. 'Yes, isn't she? Hello, Katy, I'm Claire Underwood. Take no notice of Toby, you'll soon get used to him. He always says exactly what he thinks.' She looked at Sean. 'Are you going to join us for tea, or are you in a hurry to get up to Raikeside Lodge?'

He looked at his watch. 'I think I'd better go,' he said. 'I told Kenzie I'd be there for tea and you know how she fusses if she doesn't get off in time for her husband coming home. I don't want to get into her bad books this early.'

He deposited Katy's case on the step and got back into the car. Suddenly she knew a moment of panic. He was going—leaving her with a houseful of strangers in lovely but alien surroundings. But she swallowed the feeling

78

of desolation, lifting her arm to wave to him as he drove away.

'Bye—see you tomorrow!' he called. 'Don't forget that picnic, Toby. I'll ask Kenzie if she'll make us some of her famous treacle scones, shall I?' And a moment later the yellow car was lost to view among the trees.

Claire Underwood slipped an arm around Katy's shoulders. 'I expect you're feeling a bit strange,' she said perceptively. 'I'll show you to your room and you can unpack and have a wash, then we'll have tea and you can meet Jake, my husband.' She smiled reassuringly. 'We're very informal here—no need to stand on ceremony.'

Toby ran ahead of them up the stairs. 'Can I show Katy her room? It's next to mine,' he told her. 'Can you play cricket, Katy? Can you make up stories?'

'You must allow Katy to settle in before you begin bombarding her with your demands,' Claire admonished.

The inside of the house was as lovely as its exterior. The front door opened on to a large square hall which doubled as a dining-room. An open staircase went up to a gallery off which led two rooms one of which Claire told her was the main bedroom, whilst the other was Jake's study. Katy heard the staccato tapping of a typewriter as they passed and Claire said:

'He works better here than anywhere else

79

we've been. We're so grateful to Sean for bringing this place to our notice. We used to come up to Raikeside Lodge to spend holidays with his grandfather and the peace and quiet is out of this world.' She looked anxiously at Katy. 'I do hope it won't be dull for you. There isn't much amusement except what we make for ourselves.'

Katy shook her head. 'I'm sure it could never be dull with Toby around. Anyway, I've never been to Yorkshire before and I'm looking forward to exploring.'

'Exploring! Exploring! We're going exploring!' Toby sang as he threw open a door at the end of the corridor. 'This is your room, Katy. Do you want me to help you unpack?'

'Indeed she doesn't, young man!' Claire said severely. 'She wants to have a little peace and quiet to collect herself. You can come up and tell her when tea is ready but right now you're coming downstairs with me!' She grinned at Katy. 'You'll find you have to be very firm with him. Don't let those huge innocent eyes fool you.' She pointed to a door on the far side of the room. 'That's your bathroom. I'm afraid you have to share it with Toby but I don't think you'll find that too much of a problem. His main aim in life seems to be to spend as little time in close contact with water as possible.' She laughed and ruffled Toby's dark hair. 'Come on, you

80

grubby little beast. Let Katy have five minutes to herself, then she's all yours—God help her!'

When they had gone Katy stood looking round the pleasant room. A rose-pink carpet covered the floor and the white walls were plain except for two water-colour landscapes that hung above the bed. Curtains of rose-sprigged material hung at the window and the big brass bed was prettily flounced and covered by a pale pink duvet. She went to the window and opened it, leaning out to breathe the sparkling, peat-scented air. A panorama of rising moorland stretched as far as she could see. Rabbits played quite openly on the tussocky grass whilst the sheep and their new lambs grazed serenely. She sighed. It was all so idyllic. Surely she should be able to come to some decision about her future here. Toby seemed lively enough. Not at all true to the image she had formed of a pale, wan little invalid, but as vital and full of mischief as any other little boy.

She had just finished putting away the last of her clothes in the roomy wardrobe when there was a tap on the door and Toby's voice said, 'Tea's ready, Katy.'

She opened the door and he looked admiringly at the cool green cotton dress she had changed into.

'You look nice,' he said. 'Just like a—' He screwed up his face in concentration. 'What are those flowers called?'

'A marigold?' she asked wryly.

He grinned. 'That's it. How did you know?'

She laughed and ruffled his hair. 'I've heard it before somewhere,' she told him, closing the door. 'Come on now, or you'll get us both into trouble for being late.'

The Underwoods were having tea in the drawing-room which looked on to the garden. Long windows opened on to a sheltered patio formed by the 'L' angle of the house. Claire stood up and held out her hand.

'Katy—that's better, you look refreshed. Come and meet my husband. Jake, this is Katy Lang.'

He wasn't at all what she imagined a best-selling author to look like. Tall and thin, perhaps ten years older than his wife, Jake uncoiled himself from his chair and offered her his hand. He wore shabby jeans and a sweater and his brown hair and beard badly needed a trim.

'Hello, Katy.' Dark eyes like Toby's smiled down into hers as he shook her hand warmly. 'I hope you'll be happy here and that you don't find us too overwhelming. We're a pretty bizarre lot, I'm afraid.'

'I'm sure I shall love it,' she said, warming to him. 'May I say how much I enjoyed *Devil's Country*? I'm so looking forward to reading the sequel.'

He smiled. 'I shall see to it that you have a signed copy. It's the least I can do—after all it'll be largely due to you that it gets written at all.' Katy looked puzzled and he explained, 'My publisher has given me a terrifying deadline and this young fellow has to be entertained. I can't do it till I'm finished—so—' He spread his hands and Katy nodded, latching on immediately to his message that this was the story Toby had been told to explain her presence.

After tea Jake went back to his study to work until dinner and Claire and Toby took her on a tour of the garden.

'Jake would work until he dropped if I let him,' Claire confided as Toby ran on ahead. 'Once he's worked his way inside a novel nothing else exists for him. Did you see that terrible old sweater he was wearing? He puts on the first thing that comes to hand when he gets up in the morning and I practically have to tear it off him to get it washed and mended! Mind you—' she grimaced. 'It's quite a different story when things aren't going well. Then he haunts the house like a ghost—muttering to himself, all irritable and moody.'

Katy shook her head. 'It must make life difficult at times.'

Claire smiled. 'I wouldn't have him any other way. At least life is never dull.'

They were standing at the water's edge,

under the willow trees. Suddenly Claire looked at her and asked, 'How long have you known Sean?'

The question was so unexpected that Katy found a tell-tale blush staining her cheeks. 'Oh—some time,' she said. 'He's been at St Anne's for about two years. I've been there for three.'

Claire nodded. 'I hope you don't mind, but he told me about your exam failure. I'm sorry, it was bad luck,' she said frankly. 'But it seems we have that failure to thank for your being here, so it's an ill wind. I hope you do decide to go back and try again—I know Sean does too.'

Katy shrugged. 'I don't see how it can matter to Sean what I do,' she said.

Claire looked surprised. 'Oh—but I'm sure it does. He thinks very highly of you. He wouldn't have asked you to come to us if he didn't. He and Jake have been friends for a long time.'

Katy bit her lip. 'Oh no—I didn't mean—' But Claire laid a hand on her arm.

'I think I understand, my dear. Sean can be thoughtless at times, but there's a very sincere man and a dedicated doctor under that playboy image he shows to the world.'

Back in the house Claire sent Toby off to the kitchen with a message for the cook whilst she took Katy up to his room. Taking a key from a high shelf she opened a cupboard.

'This is where I put all the things that Sean supplied us with,' she said. 'They look so grim. I didn't want Toby to see them and be frightened. Once these attacks of his pass off he seems to forget all about them and I don't want him to have constant reminders staring him in the face.'

In the cupboard there was an oxygen cylinder and mask, the peak-flow meter and chart Sean had explained that he wanted her to use each day and a pile of extra pillows. Katy took the key from Claire and slipped it into her pocket.

'He may appear to have forgotten all about his asthma but I doubt very much if he has,' she said. 'And once he knows what these things are for they could make him feel more secure. Sean wants us to use the peak-flow meter every night and morning so Toby will have to get used to that anyway.'

Claire smiled. 'I never looked at it in that way. Now I come to think of it I suppose it could be a comfort to him to know that help is near if he needs it.' She sighed. 'Of course it has been reassuring to have negative results on all the tests that Sean has arranged so far but Jake and I would give anything to know the cause of these cruel attacks—and why Toby's asthma suddenly returned.'

'It's often very difficult to pin down,' Katy told her. 'But I'm sure that if anyone can do it, Sean can—and of course I'll help all I can.'

After Claire had gone Katy opened the communicating door between her room and Toby's, so that he could wander in if he wanted to, then she began to arrange her belongings around the room. She was just sitting Arnold in his customary place on the pillow when she looked up to see Toby standing hesitantly in the doorway.

'You can come in if you like,' she told him.

He came in, looking round eagerly at her collection of china animals, then he turned to the bed.

'You've still got a teddy!'

'Of course,' she said. 'I couldn't go anywhere without him. He's as old as I am and his name is Arnold. Do you like him?'

He nodded thoughtfully. 'I thought that people over the age of six weren't allowed teddies. I had one once but when I went away to school I wasn't allowed to take him. When I came home he'd gone.'

'Oh—what a shame.' Privately Katy wondered what unimaginative person had done that. Aloud she said: 'Well, I wouldn't like to be without mine. I'm glad he didn't go away.' She sat down on the bed and Toby joined her, his thin little legs sticking straight out in front of him. She picked up Arnold and gave him to the little boy.

'Shall I tell you a secret that I've never told anyone else?' she whispered.

He looked up eagerly. 'Yes please.'

'Well, when I was your age I couldn't say my prayers without hugging Arnold. I used to think he was like a sort of telephone to God and that he could help all my dreams to come true.'

'And do you still think that?' He stared solemnly at her.

She shook her head. 'No. I know now that if you want something very badly and you keep trying hard there's a good chance that you'll get it in the end. But it does help sometimes to have someone like Arnold to hang on to.' She looked at Toby as he sat there wistfully stroking the almost threadbare teddy. 'Poor Arnold. I've loved almost all his fur off over the years. Tell you what—would you like him to live in your room while I'm here?'

He looked up at her in amazement. 'Could he really? Don't you mind?'

She laughed. 'Not at all. I can tell he likes you.'

Dinner was a relaxed meal at which Toby joined them, dressed in his dressing-gown, ready for bed. As soon as it was over Claire insisted that he went up and Katy accompanied him, tucking Arnold in beside him and promising that they'd be up bright and early next morning ready for the picnic with Sean.

Downstairs in the dining-room Claire was playing the grand piano that stood in the corner by the large open fireplace. She played well, her fingers rippling over the keys in melodies from recent hit musicals. Katy sat down quietly in a corner to listen. Jake sat by the window, scribbling in a notebook, and suddenly he looked up and suggested some Chopin. Immediately Claire began to play the Minute Waltz and Katy was riveted by her skill.

As the last notes died away she was about to make a congratulatory remark when another sound caught her attention, making her look up. At the top of the stairs a small figure in a dressing-gown stood looking down at them, white faced and shaking with the paroxysms of coughing he was unable to control. As he fought for breath Toby clutched at the banister rails. Katy took the stairs two at a time, Jake and Claire following.

'He has an inhaler,' Claire said as they reached the landing. 'It's in the drawer of his bedside table.'

Katy scooped the little boy up in her arms and carried him to his room. She found the inhaler and helped him to use it, propping extra pillows behind him on the bed. Holding his hand tightly she reasured him smilingly.

'That's right, Toby. Try to breathe deeply and relax. It'll be all right in a minute.'

'Do you need the oxygen?' Jake asked anxiously, but Katy shook her head.

'I don't think so—not this time.'

Slowly Toby's spasm left him. The anxiety in the dark eyes lessened and Katy noticed the muscles around his neck relax. She motioned to Jake and Claire who were hovering nervously in the doorway that the crisis was over, then she went to the cupboard and fetched the peak-flow meter and chart. This seemed as good a moment as any to explain its use to Toby.

'This is a kind of game your Uncle Sean wants us to play each night and morning,' she said. 'It's a good game because it tells us when one of your nasty turns is likely to occur so that he can do something to help stop them.' She showed him the meter with its circular dial and mouthpiece. 'See—you blow in here and the dial shows us just how hard you are able to push the air out, then we have to write it down on this chart.' She smiled at him. 'Shall we have a go with it now?'

Toby obligingly blew into the mouthpiece and Katy recorded the expected low reading on the chart and put it away again in the cupboard. Toby's breathing seemed easier and she took away one of his pillows and settled him for sleep. He reached out to grasp her hand.

'Don't go, Katy,' he begged.

'All right, I'll sit here for a while, but you must go to sleep soon or you'll never wake in time for the picnic in the morning.' She tucked him in and sat down at the bedside.

'Katy,' he whispered. 'If I hug Arnold very tightly every night for a whole month, do you think he might make my cough go away?'

She smiled. 'Well, you never know. He's done some very wonderful things in his life.'

She watched as the big brown eyes closed tightly. She could still hear the gentle rasping of his laboured breath and her heart went out to him. Already the little boy had captured quite a large corner of her heart.

## CHAPTER SEVEN

Katy held the peak-flow meter to Toby's lips while he blew into it as hard as he could. A glance at the dial told her that his air output was almost back to normal and she smiled as she filled in the am half of the chart.

'Great! No nasty turns today. Hurry and get up now. Your Uncle Sean will be here before we've had breakfast if we're not quick.'

He scrambled out of bed. 'It works!' he told her excitedly. 'I hugged Arnold hard and he made it better!'

They had just finished breakfast when a loud hooting from outside told them that Sean had arrived. With a whoop of delight Toby ran to the door to greet him, his father following.

Claire looked at Katy. 'Better take some extra woollies in case the weather changes,' she said. 'The sky looks clear enough but it can be unpredictable up here at this time of year.'

When Katy rejoined them on the drive the family were talking and laughing with Sean and she hung back, not wanting to intrude. Sean looked relaxed and handsome this morning, dressed casually in jeans and a roll-neck sweater. On the back seat of the car was a picnic hamper and she saw that he too had brought extra clothes. Toby was bouncing up and down in the car, impatient to be off and when he saw her he shouted,

'Come on, Katy! Tell Uncle Sean it's time to go. He won't listen to me.'

The others laughed and Jake turned to smile at her, drawing her into the little circle. 'I'm afraid poor Katy has been rather thrown in at the deep end,' he said quietly, putting an arm casually across her shoulders. 'And coped extremely well, if I may say so. But she'll tell you all about that herself, no doubt.' He slapped Sean on the shoulder. 'It's good to see you. What a pity we're both up here to work. You must come to dinner with us as soon as you can.' He glanced at Claire ruefully. 'Right now it's back to the grindstone for me. Have a good time. See you later.'

91

He and Claire waved as the car made its way down the drive, between the flowering shrubs. They drove through the white gates and on to the road to cross the bridge and climb the village road up towards the moors.

'Where are we going, Uncle Sean?' Toby wanted to know.

'Belldon Cross Caverns,' Sean told him with a smile. 'You've never been down a real cave, have you?'

'No—super!' Toby wriggled with excitement on the back seat. 'How far is it? When will we get there?'

'It's not too far. Just you sit still and wait. Tell you what—see how many sheep you can count with black faces. That'll help to pass the time.' Sean turned to Katy. 'I take it you've settled in then?'

She nodded. 'The Underwoods are very nice, they've made me feel very welcome.'

'And you had a spot of bother last night, I hear.'

She shook her head. 'It wasn't serious—perhaps just the excitement. I've started recording the peak-flow readings, by the way. I tried to explain it to Toby and he treats it as a game. Claire says that once his attacks are over he quickly forgets all about them.'

He nodded. 'A typical characteristic of most asthmatics. They seem determined to live as normally as possible—even driving

92

themselves to do things they know quite well they can't manage. But I suppose that's better than giving in.'

They had reached the top of the moor by now and the wind whistled round the car. The view took Katy's breath away; miles of rolling moorland as far as the eye could see, craggy with rocks in places, the outcrops standing like ruined castles against the clear blue of the sky. They had reached the highest spot when Sean drew the car off the road on to a smooth plateau that dropped precipitously away into a valley where the ubiquitous sheep calmly cropped the coarse grass. He turned to the small, excited boy in the back.

'Right—this is it. Shall we go?'

The caverns were a local tourist attraction, but as it was so early in the season they had only just opened. The smiling woman in the hut that served as a paybox told them that they were the first visitors of the day and asked if they could manage without a guide. Sean laughed.

'I know these caves like the back of my own hand,' he said. 'My grandfather used to bring me here for a special treat in the school holidays.'

They entered the caves through an opening in the rocks, down a narrow stairway cut into the stone. Katy felt a small hand grasp hers and whispered, 'All right, Toby?'

The large brown eyes looked up into hers and she felt him shiver slightly as he whispered back,

'Yes—it's creepy though, isn't it?'

At the bottom the caves were flooded with electric lights, carefully concealed to bring out the beauty of the mineral formation without being obviously artificial. Toby stared around him in wonder at the stalactites glowing and sparkling with pink and green crystals and the stalagmites rising up from the floor in strange shapes like fairy castles. Sean told him the story of how the formations had grown year by year out of the sediments left by dripping water.

'Some of them were here when dinosaurs roamed over the moors,' he told the little boy who was listening with eyes that grew rounder by the minute. 'Maybe there was one living in this very cave. What a tale these rocks could tell us if they could only speak!'

At last they came out into the sunlight again and got back into the car to drive to a more gentle part of the moor where Toby could play with his ball. Sean looked at Katy.

'I've brought a rug. Do you think it's warm enough to eat outside? The wind has turned very cool.' He stood looking out over the moor, shading his eyes with one hand. 'Mmm—I don't like the look of that bank of cloud on the horizon,' he said. 'It can be very treacherous up here. I'll just give Toby a quick game of football, then I think we'd better be moving.'

Katy tried to see the bank of cloud he was looking at but it didn't look very menacing to her. The sun was shining so brightly surely the worst they could have was a spring shower. She had to admit that the wind had turned cold though, and she soon went back to the car to pull a warm sweater on over her shirt and jeans so that she could watch Toby and Sean at their football in comfort. Today she was seeing yet another facet of Sean's personality. He seemed every little boy's idea of the perfect uncle, yet she knew that all the time he was observing Toby carefully, watching for the least sign of breathlessness or fatigue.

By the time they returned to the car she had unpacked the picnic hamper and arranged the food as best she could. Toby had obviously worked up an appetite, attacking his meal with relish and exclaiming over Sean's housekeeper's melt-in-the-mouth cookery. Katy had to agree. The pasties, scones and tarts she had made would have done credit to a royal chef. She told Sean so and he smiled.

'Kenzie used to work for my grandfather. He and Granny brought her with them when they first moved here from Scotland thirty years ago. She was a young woman then and she's lived in Yorkshire longer than she was ever across the border yet she's as much a Scot now as ever she was, bless her.'

Katy smiled. 'I'd like to meet her—and get some of her recipes if she'd give them to me.'

'So you shall.' Sean glanced up at the sky again. 'In fact maybe sooner than you think. I've a feeling we'd do well to get down off the moors as soon as we can. That storm is coming this way fast now.'

There was a disappointed wail from the back of the car, 'Oh no, Uncle Sean! I want to stay here and hunt for dinosaurs.'

But already Sean was switching on the ignition. 'If we stay here much longer you'll find yourself here all night, young man,' he said grimly. 'And believe me, you wouldn't like that one little bit!'

'Can we go to your house then?' Toby begged. 'It isn't time to go home yet and Katy did say she'd like to meet Kenzie.'

Sean hesitated, looking at Katy. 'What do you say—would you like that?'

She nodded. 'Yes, I would—very much indeed.'

As they drove Sean told them that the house his grandfather had left him had once been owned by a man who also owned a stone quarry high on the moors. It was called Raikeside Lodge because it was built close to the narrow walled road that led up to the quarry—the kind of road known locally as a 'raikes'.

'No doubt he built it there so that he could keep an eye on his quarrymen,' Sean laughed. 'To make sure they clocked on in good time in the morning and didn't shirk.'

'Can I see the quarry?' Toby asked excitedly.

'We'll have to see if the weather holds,' Sean said. 'It's worked out now but I have heard that the stone that made up the first railway platforms came from there. Cutting and splitting into those huge slabs was a work of art. You can still see the little railway they used and there are still some old tools in a hut there.'

Toby was wriggling on his seat with excitement, his disappointment at having to leave the moors quite forgotten.

As they drove Katy began to see that Sean had been right about the weather. The heavy bank of cloud had moved fast and now it was almost overhead. The sun had gone and a cold unfriendly wind was growing stronger by the minute, whistling eerily across the vast empty space. Rain, then sleet began to lash the windscreen, then, to Katy's amazement, the sleet gave way to flakes of snow. She saw now the reason for Sean's insistence that they should get away.

'Maybe we'd better postpone our visit to your house for today,' she said, turning to him. 'Perhaps you could drop us off as you go through the village.'

He shook his head. 'We're not going that way. I'm driving north. Yesterday I made a slight detour to drop you at Belldon Cross. But don't worry, we'll soon be there now.' He glanced at her anxious face as she peered through the windscreen at the sheep huddled against the drystone walls, their fleeces already caked with snow. 'Incredible, isn't it? I did warn you though. Just when you think summer has come this can happen to bring you back to earth. That's Yorkshire for you!'

'Surely it can't last long in May?' she said, looking at him.

'No. Once the storm has passed it'll soon clear up and thaw, but it can be very nasty for anyone unfortunate enough to be caught in it.'

They turned off the road to drive for about a mile down a narrow lane, then Katy saw the house, perched halfway up the rise on a knoll. The road leading to it was so steep that Sean had to make several tries at it, the wheels of the car slipping on the wet snow. But at last they reached the top and Katy got out to look over the magnificent wild view that lay below them. But the weather precluded any standing and staring and Sean soon hustled them inside the low stone house. Katy had a first impression of stone-flagged floors and oak-panelled walls, gleaming copper and dark red stair-carpet. The homely scents of furniture polish and lavender filled the air.

98

Sean opened a door and ushered them inside a room with a low beamed ceiling. It was furnished with comfortable, well-worn leather chairs, and a heavy antique desk stood in the window. In the wide stone fireplace a wood fire crackled behind a fireguard.

'This is my den,' he told them. 'It's where I work. Warm yourselves at the fire and I'll go and see if Kenzie can rustle us up some tea.' But he was back a moment later with a scrap of paper in his hand. 'Kenzie has had to go home. She left me this note,' he explained. 'But she's left food enough to feed the entire Mackenzie clan so we'll be all right.'

'Oh, she doesn't live in then?' Katy asked.

He shook his head. 'She used to but she married a local shepherd ten years ago. No doubt her husband will be worried about his new lambs in this weather and Kenzie has gone off to have a meal ready for him when he gets in.' He rubbed his hands and held them out to the blazing logs. Katy looked hesitantly at him.

'I'll go and make the tea, if you're sure she won't mind another woman in her kitchen,' she offered.

The three of them drank tea and toasted muffins in front of the log fire whilst outside the snow continued to fall, making a soft whisper against the glass. Toby thought it all a marvellous adventure but after a while Katy looked at her watch, then at the darkening sky outside.

'What are we going to do about getting back to Bridge House?' she asked. 'Mrs Underwood must be wondering where we are.'

Sean walked to the window and looked out. 'The snow's stopped but it's still very cold. I'm afraid the roads will be bad now until morning,' he said doubtfully. 'Quite honestly I can't see myself negotiating that hill tonight.' He turned to look at them. 'I can't see anything else for it—you'll have to stay the night. I'll ring Claire and let her know.'

'Hooray!' Toby jumped wildly up and down with delight. 'Then you can show me the quarry in the morning can't you, Uncle Sean?'

Sean laughed as he dialled the number. 'I don't see why not.' His eyes met Katy's and held them for a moment. For a split second her heart seemed to stand still as she tried to read the enigmatic message she saw in them, then his expression changed abruptly as Claire answered the telephone.

In the cosy kitchen, warmed by the huge, old-fashioned range, they ate the delicious casserole left for them by Sean's housekeeper, washed down by mugs of hot coffee and followed by crusty home-made bread and farmhouse cheese.

Afterwards Sean gave Toby a piggyback ride up to bed in the room he had occupied himself as a small boy. As Katy tucked him into the big feather bed between lavender-scented sheets he sighed happily.

'Hasn't it been a *super* day?' he said. 'I do wish I'd brought Arnold with me.' He reached up to wind his arms around her neck, hugging her hard. 'I'm glad you came to Yorkshire to stay with us,' he told her, his eyelids already drooping. 'And I can't *wait* till tomorrow—can you?'

Katy closed the door of his room softly and stood for a moment on the landing. All day Sean had been at his most formal with her; the relationship between them friendly, but cool and professional—just as he had promised. But the look in his eyes as he had waited for Claire to answer the telephone had quickened her heartbeat. Now she was remembering the things said about him by the other nurses at St Anne's, the stories that had circulated, growing, she suspected, in exaggeration as they passed from mouth to mouth. Now that Toby was in bed and they were virtually alone together would he try to take advantage of the situation—or did he really see her as a 'frightened little girl'? Someone he found amusing but not in the least challenging? She hardly knew which prospect she feared more.

Downstairs in the cosy, shabby den Sean had stoked the fire with apple logs. It hissed and popped cosily, spurting out darts of flame

101

to light the room which was illuminated by one small reading lamp only. Katy stood in the doorway, trying to imagine Sean working away at the desk in the window, cluttered with papers and medical textbooks. He stood at a carved oak cupboard in the corner of the room, pouring brandy, and as she closed the door he turned to smile at her, holding out the decanter. She shook her head but he poured her a generous measure all the same.

'To keep out the cold,' he said, handing her the balloon glass. 'It's been a strange day for you. Your first taste of the real Yorkshire—beautiful and unpredictable. Calm and serene one minute, vicious and ruthless the next.'

Katy nodded. 'I can see now where the Brontë sisters got all their inspiration from.'

He stretched his length in an armchair by the fire, smiling lazily up at her. 'Come and sit down—no, not there—' as she took a seat on the opposite side of the hearth. 'Closer—where I can see the firelight on that hair of yours.'

She shook her head. 'I—I'm perfectly all right here, thank you.'

He shrugged. 'Just as you please, but we've a good few hours to pass together, we might as well relax with each other, don't you think?'

He was looking at her in a way she found almost unbearable, his eyes twinkling as though he knew quite well how uncomfortable she was. She sipped her brandy and felt the fiery warmth of it spread through her veins, easing the tension. 'I can be friendly quite easily from here,' she said. 'I don't see why—'

'Katy—are you afraid of me?' he interrupted. 'I mean afraid of being alone with me like this? Am I so very formidable? Have you been listening to tales about me—is that it?'

She shook her head, her cheeks flaming, giving the lie to the gesture.

He laughed gently. 'Poor Katy, what can they have been saying?' Suddenly his voice hardened. 'Oh don't be so ridiculous, girl! Come and sit here.'

She was shocked into obedience by the sudden command and before she knew what she was doing she had risen to her feet. His hand shot out to grasp hers, pulling her down on to a large floor cushion at his feet.

'That's better.' He leaned back in his chair, letting one hand remain on her shoulder. 'You know Katy, people are like diamonds,' he said thoughtfully. 'Each one of us has many facets and we're never quite the same with two people alike—some people bring out the best in us, some the worst. Each new person we meet brings out another dimension. Today I've seen the Katy that Toby brings out in you. I liked her, but I'm still waiting to meet my Katy. So far you seem to switch yourself off when I'm around. I'd like very much to know why that is.'

She took another sip of her brandy, wondering how to answer his question. 'As far as I know I'm exactly the same with everyone,' she said at last.

'Come now, you can't mean that,' he said. 'I'm not talking about the way you're supposed to behave professionally, as a nurse, but how you respond emotionally. While you were out of the room Toby was telling me how much he likes you. He was telling me about—what's his name—Arthur?'

She blushed. 'Arnold—only the old teddy bear you saw Isobel throw at me. I gave him to Toby because he liked him—that's all.'

'There, you see what I mean? You've clammed up on me,' he said triumphantly. 'You described him to Toby as your oldest friend and confidante.'

She shook her head impatiently. 'One speaks differently to a child, of course. That doesn't mean anything!'

'Ah but you see I think it does,' he insisted. 'Perhaps we're more truthful with children. For instance, didn't you tell Toby that if one wants something very badly and tries very hard one usually gets that thing in the end?'

She twisted her head to look up at him. 'He told you that I said that?'

'Yes, he did. It impressed him very much.

104

The point is, Katy, if you believe that, why are you running away from nursing?'

She shrugged. 'That's simple—because I'm no longer sure it's what I do want.' As she turned her head away she felt his fingers lace into her hair, turning her face towards him again.

'I don't think I believe that,' he told her. 'But if it is true, then what *do* you want from life?'

His eyes were burning into hers and she tried to free herself but his fingers held her hair firmly, making it painful to move. 'I wanted to go home, to care for my father,' she said stiffly. 'You already know that—you also know that the situation has changed. Now I have to re-think.'

For a long moment he looked at her till she said quietly, 'Will you let go of my hair, please—you're hurting me.'

He released his hold on her hair without an apology, but moved his hand down to the curve of her neck, his fingers lying along her jawline. 'You're not really so appalled at the idea of your father marrying again, are you?' he asked quietly.

She shook her head. 'I suppose not. It's just the difference in age.'

'Is it because you feel that Isobel will replace you in your father's affections? Are you so dependent on him still? Has there never been anyone you wanted for yourself?'

She turned to stare at him, frowning slightly. 'Damn it, Katy—I'm asking you if you've ever been in love—can't you understand that?'

She scrambled to her feet and stared down angrily at him. 'The things you're asking are none of your business,' she exploded. 'I did what you asked in accepting this job—what more do you want of me?'

He stood up hastily to face her. 'I want us to be friends, Katy. I'm sorry if what I said upset you.' He took her shoulders and pulled her gently towards him. 'Please—'

She bit her lip, suddenly dangerously close to tears. 'You seem to enjoy finding my weakest, most vulnerable spots and probing them,' she said bitterly. 'If you really want to know, I suppose I resent Isobel for taking my mother's place—now that I've said it, it sounds stupid and childish. As for being in love—I believe that real love has to grow, slowly, like a tree. All that romantic stuff in books—I just don't believe in it.'

Very gently he slid his arms around her, drawing her close as his mouth found hers. With one hand he pulled the pins from her hair and the glowing auburn mass tumbled about her shoulders. When he lifted his head to look down at her she was slightly breathless, her eyes wide and her mouth trembling. The hand that had loosened her hair cupped her chin, tilting her face upwards as he looked into her eyes.

'I don't think you have the least idea how very desirable you are, Katy,' he said. 'Underneath all that fierce independence you're so vulnerable—so sweetly fragile. You make me want to—'

His lips found hers again and Katy gave up all ideas of fighting him, surrendering herself to the rush of feeling that overwhelmed her. With a kind of wonder she realised that in spite of what she had just said it *was* true—all the excitement, the shattering sensation she had read of in books was happening to her right now, at this moment. The brief relationships she had had in the past paled into insignificance as she gave herself up to Sean's insistent mouth, her own melting beneath it, flowering to allow the intimate caress of his gently exploring tongue.

'You see,' he whispered against her cheek. 'You're wrong, so wrong, Katy darling. You know it now, don't you?' He smiled down at her. 'You're like a little glow-worm, all golden and sparkling.' He pulled her down with him on to the huge cushion before the smouldering fire, leaning back against the armchair and cradling her against his chest. 'So this is the Katy that shines for me,' he said teasingly, kissing her again. 'Mmm—I approve.' His lips lingered against hers, then moved to her ear and the hollow beneath it. She shivered slightly as his lips moved to the base of her throat and as her head fell back she felt his fingers in her hair again, cradling her head whilst with his other hand he began to undo the buttons of her shirt. His fingers were warm and firm against her flesh, seductive and caressing as they moved the thin material aside to bare one shoulder. His lips moved against the coolness of her skin, sending shivers of ecstasy through her as she leaned her cheek against the roughness of his hair.

'You're perfect, Katy,' he whispered. 'The perfect mixture of fire and ice. You excite me more than any other woman I know. Darling, I want you so much.'

His lips took hers again, this time with a passion and urgency that both thrilled and terrified her. Her senses swam and she felt her control slipping away. As she returned his kiss every instinct she possessed urged her to surrender—to allow herself to be swept along on the surging current of passion Sean aroused in her, but right at the back of her mind a small insistent voice warned her to remember the stories that had circulated at St Anne's. *'If he meant anything he said he would have married and settled down long ago.'* She could hear Sonia saying it now. *'He's just a playboy who enjoys playing the field. Anyone who gets into his clutches had better be playing the same game or prepare to be hurt!'* Katy didn't want to be hurt. Already she could feel herself falling helplessly in love. She mustn't—*wouldn't* allow him to take her heart and tear it to shreds just to pass an otherwise boring evening!

Panicking, she pushed him from her and sat up, straightening her disarranged shirt and hair with trembling fingers. Sean stared at her, his eyes concerned.

'Katy—darling, what is it—what's the matter?' He reached out to touch her face.

For a moment he looked so sincere that she almost relented and hurled herself back into his arms, but her strong will prevailed. She scrambled to her feet so as to get as far away from his disturbing closeness as she could.

'I—it's getting late,' she said inadequately.

He got quickly to his feet and put his arms around her. 'You *are* afraid, aren't you? Darling, don't you trust me? Don't say you don't feel as I do Katy, because I can feel it when I hold you like this—the way your heart beats, the softness of your lips.' He looked down at her but she refused to meet his eyes.

'I—can't explain. Please, Sean—don't ask me to.'

But he wouldn't let her go. 'Are you afraid of committing yourself? You needn't be. You could still be perfectly free. I don't believe in two people being tied to each other—trapped. That's not what love is about at all in my book.'

She tore herself away from him. 'But it is in

109

mine! I can't help it—don't you see?' Her eyes blazed at him. 'It's all right for people like you who can turn their feelings on and off at will! I'm not like that—and I never want to be, so there's an end to it!'

There was a long silence as they stared at each other. Katy's heart sank as she saw his eyes cloud and harden. She had said what she meant—what she felt she had to say—but somehow it had sounded all wrong—prudish and self-righteous. She opened her mouth to try to put it right and then closed it again hopelessly, biting her lip in anguish.

Sean lifted his shoulders resignedly. 'I misjudged you, Katy. I'm sorry.' He glanced at his watch. 'You're right—it is late. Better get some sleep.' And without another word he walked past her and out of the room.

She felt as though someone had thrown iced-water over her. Her heart froze. It was as if she had opened a door to glimpse something beautiful and then slammed it and turned the key. Was she a complete fool—a naïve, simplistic fool?

Far into the stormy night, as the wind and rain lashed against her bedroom window, Katy lay wrestling with the same question. Nowadays people took what they wanted from life when the opportunity presented itself, often they tossed it aside when they had done with it. Maybe that was the right way—better to take what one could than miss out altogether. But could a happiness that was so short-lived leave one with anything but a broken heart? She wished she knew the answer.

Dawn was already breaking when at last she admitted to herself that already it was too late—she was too much in love with Sean not to be hurt now, anyway.

## CHAPTER EIGHT

Katy arrived downstairs in the kitchen next morning to find Toby talking animatedly to a stout, grey-haired woman in a print overall. As she came in he turned to her.

'Oh, there you are, Katy! I tried to wake you but you were fast asleep. This is Kenzie. She's making us some breakfast.'

'Good morning,' Katy smiled at the woman. 'You must be wondering what we're doing here.'

The Scotswoman shook her head, smiling. 'Not at all. Mr Sean has been up and about these two hours. He told me how you were caught in the storm yesterday.' She clicked her tongue. 'A real brute, wasn't it? Yet this morning you'd never have guessed it could have raged like that. Apart from a few patches of snow on the tops there's no sign of it.' She shovelled golden-yolked eggs on to

111

plates warming at the side of the range. 'This morning those moors have the innocence of a babe, yet my man had his work cut out with the ewes and lambs last night.'

'Thank you for breakfast,' Katy said gratefully. 'And I hope Toby hasn't been getting in your way.'

'That he hasn't, bless him.' Kenzie smiled. 'It's a treat to have a bairn about the house again. I've half promised to take him up to see the lambs when I take my man's dinner later on.'

'Well, I don't know,' Katy said doubtfully. 'We should be getting back to Bridge House really. Toby's mother will be worrying.'

'Oh, Katy!' Toby wailed. 'She won't worry. And Uncle Sean said he'd take me up to the old quarry. We can go home after lunch.' He looked appealingly at Kenzie. 'You don't mind, do you?'

Katy looked at the huge brown eyes, feeling herself weaken. Kenzie smiled at her over Toby's head as she put the loaded plates in front of them. 'I'm afraid you're on a loser this time, Miss Lang. I'm thinking those eyes will be breaking a few hearts one of these fine days. Maybe you'd better ring Mrs Underwood and tell her you'll be home this afternoon.'

'But won't it put you out?' Katy asked.

The housekeeper shook her head. 'Bless you, no. It's no more work to cook for three

112

than for one and it's nice to have a bit of company. It can get mighty lonely up here, you know.'

When she had eaten the last of her breakfast Katy made her way to the den to telephone Bridge House. She opened the door, then stopped as she saw Sean seated at his desk working quietly, his books open before him. He looked up.

'Good morning. Come in.'

'Good morning—I didn't know you were in here or I wouldn't have disturbed you. I was going to ring Claire to tell her we'd be home this afternoon. Toby insists that you and he are going up to the old quarry and Kenzie has promised him a trip to see the new lambs too.'

He laughed. 'He seems to have planned the day for you! Of course—help yourself to the phone.'

'I'm a bit concerned over Toby's chest,' she confided. 'I haven't got his PF meter with me, though I must say he seems all right at the moment.'

'He'll be fine,' Sean assured her. 'I don't want you to make too much of a thing of the PF records. It could defeat the whole object.' He frowned. 'If we could only find a common factor that triggers off the attacks.'

Katy made her call to Bridge House and as she put down the receiver Sean looked up and said,

'Are you coming up to the quarry with Toby and me? It's a beautiful morning, you'll enjoy it.'

She nodded. 'Thank you, yes I'd like to.' It was as though last night had never happened.

It was a steep climb up to the quarry but although Toby got quite out of breath it didn't stop him from chattering all the way.

'Kenzie's husband's got two dogs—one's called Gyp and the other one's Flash. I'm going with her when we get back, to take them their dinner. Do you know that he has to dig the sheep and lambs out of the snow sometimes, but their woolly coats are so thick that they don't feel the cold—and they can live for a long time without eating too—because of the fat under their skins.'

Katy studied Sean's face, her heart lurching a little. Did he despise her—think of her as stupid and naïve? The phrase 'frightened little girl' rang mockingly in her ears again and she hated herself for being so gauche. Why couldn't she have been like any other girl and enjoyed his lovemaking simply and lightheartedly? The answer to that was too painful to think about and she pushed it to the back of her mind. If he had found her exciting and desirable last night he must be sorely disillusioned by now. She winced as she remembered the panicky rejection—her awkward handling of the situation. Hadn't he admitted as much when he'd said 'I'm sorry.

114

I misjudged you, Katy.' Her heart was like lead in her chest.

The quarry was fascinating. A huge scar in the hillside, partly grown over with grass and bracken now, but still at the heart of it the exposed limestone shone out starkly. Toby was delighted with the rusting railway lines and the crumbling trucks, even more so with the workmans' hut and its collection of primitive tools.

'I suppose I should really donate them to a museum,' Sean said thoughtfully. 'The fact is that I haven't had much time to sort things out up here yet. My grandfather only died six months ago. To tell the truth I'm loath to change things. The place feels so empty without him as it is.'

Katy looked at him. For a second his face was wistful and vulnerable and she guessed that his grandfather had meant a great deal to him. She longed to put her hand into his as a gesture of comfort and understanding, but he seemed so remote today. Suddenly he turned to her.

'Shall we climb to the top of the scar up there? There's a magnificent view from the top. Or do you think we should be getting back?'

Katy looked at the steep climb and shook her head doubtfully. Better not to push their luck. Toby had done very well as it was. Toby read her expression and began to

115

protest.

'Oh, Katy—come on, don't be a spoilsport.'

'It's the time I'm thinking about,' she said diplomatically. 'Shepherds have their lunch early you know, and you wouldn't want to get back and find Kenzie had had to go without you.'

As they made their way back down the track Sean smiled at her. 'Ten out of ten for a neat diversion.' He reached out his hand to help her over a rocky patch, still slippery with melted snow. As his fingers touched hers her heart quickened. The sudden smile and words of approval, the casual touch of his hand—she would have to be content with these crumbs now, she told herself unhappily. Her foot slipped on the wet rock and his arm went impulsively round her waist to steady her. She looked up at him and their eyes met.

'Katy—I want you to know that I understand,' he told her quietly. 'Don't worry—and please don't look so embarrassed.' He smiled. 'We are still friends, aren't we?'

She nodded, her heart sinking even lower. What did he mean when he said he understood? How could he when she didn't herself? The very last thing she wanted to be was his friend. The fact that he wasn't annoyed with her could only mean one thing—that what had happened had been

116

unimportant to him.

On the way back she was silent, feeling awkward and miserable—unable to think of anything to say that didn't sound empty or foolish. But Toby more than made up for her silence, chattering away nineteen to the dozen. Back at the house Sean offered to accompany him and Kenzie to the moorside, leaving Katy time to get ready for the trip home to Bridge House.

It was half past two when they drove in through the gates and up the drive. As they came in sight of the house it was Toby who saw the car first.

'Wow! Look at that, Uncle Sean,' he shouted. 'It's yellow, like yours!'

Katy heard Sean draw in his breath sharply. 'Yellow it may be, but there the resemblance ends!'

The car that stood gleaming in front of the house was a sleek Mercedes and as they drew up behind it Claire came out on to the porch with a tall blonde girl. Toby cried out again, 'It's Auntie Helen!' He leapt out of the car and ran to meet her.

Katy looked at the tall, cool figure dressed so elegantly in a cream linen suit and wished that she had had more time to spend on her own appearance. This beautiful girl made her feel like a scruffy teenager in the crumpled jeans and sweater she had worn yesterday.

Claire came forward to meet them. 'So you

117

came home at last!' She laughed. 'What a storm. I must admit that Jake and I were quite worried till we got your phone call.' She held out her hand to the newcomer. 'Helen—come and meet Sean MacInnon. Sean, this is Helen Kent. She is fashion editor of *Tomorrow's Woman* and it was through her that I met Jake—I think you could say that that puts her in the category of "best friend".' She laughed as she turned her attention to Katy. 'And this is Katy Lang who is here to keep an eye on our little horror for the summer.'

Katy found herself looking at a perfect oval face, expertly made-up and with stunning eyes of deep violet-blue. Tall and slim, she seemed to tower over Katy, but the smile she gave her was warm and friendly.

'Hello. I've been hearing all about you. I hope you've recovered from your ordeal in the blizzards yesterday.'

'Yes—thank you,' Katy mumbled. She was longing to go up to her room and change, acutely aware of the untidy state of her hair and her make-up-free, scrubbed face.

Toby was prattling on, making up for any awkward silences. 'We've had a *lovely* time! We stayed the night at Uncle Sean's and I slept in the bed he used to have when he was a little boy. This morning Kenzie took me to see the baby lambs and we went to the quarry too—yesterday we had muffins for tea and cam—camisole for dinner. It was scrummy!'

Katy stood back as they all laughed. She had seen the admiring look Sean had given Helen as he shook hands with her and she couldn't really blame him. It was a long time since she had seen a more elegant woman.

'Sean—you will stay for dinner, won't you,' Claire asked him.

'Well, yes, that would be very nice.'

'I hoped you'd say yes. We're having a special treat—Scotch salmon. Helen brought it. She's on her way back from a fishing holiday in Scotland with friends. She actually caught this one herself.'

Sean smiled at Helen. 'That was very clever of you.'

'I'd like to think so, but I'm afraid the gillie did most of the work. Still, it was on my line and it did weigh nine pounds, so I suppose I deserve some congratulations.'

Claire was ushering them all inside. 'Mrs Benson has her *Mrs Beeton* out on the kitchen table and a very determined look in her eye so I believe we can look forward to something spectacular,' she laughed.

In the privacy of her room Katy took a long look at herself in the mirror. How could she ever have taken Sean's remarks seriously? She wondered if she had imagined the things he said to her last night. Certainly at the moment she looked far from exciting or desirable. Tousled hair escaping in all directions, baggy

119

sweater and frayed jeans. Angrily she tore them off and went through to the bathroom to run a bath. Claire had assured her that Toby would be fully occupied for the rest of the afternoon and that she should have some time to herself. She heard voices floating up from the garden and looking out of the window she saw Sean and Helen walking across the lawn together towards the river's edge. Anguish gnawed her heart. They looked so handsome together—almost the same height, Sean so dark and Helen so fair. As she watched, Sean threw back his head and laughed. Katy bit her lip. He was laughing *with* Helen—not *at* her. She could imagine the conversation—sparklingly witty with a hint of sophisticated flirtation.

Later she made sure that Toby had his bath and looked presentable for dinner, then she changed into the most sophisticated thing she possessed—a black velvet skirt and a lace top. She dressed her hair in the smoothest chignon she could persuade it into and made up her face with the utmost care. But even as she stood back critically to regard the result she had to admit that never in a million years could she hope to compete with the elegant Helen.

Toby bounded into the room and stopped short. 'Crumbs! You look like a stick of liquorice with a cherry on top!' he said with characteristic candour.

When Mrs Benson made her triumphal entrance with the salmon there were gasps of surprise and delight. The fish lay gleaming and silver on its oval platter, surrounded by a garnish of juicy tomato and glossy green watercress. To accompany it there were the very first new potatoes, sweetcorn and asparagus and to follow, a home-made ice-cream confection laced with pineapple and brandy. As the coffee was brought in Sean leaned back with a sigh.

'I feel as though I shan't want to eat another crumb for a month! Many thanks for inviting me to share such a feast, Claire. It really has been a treat.' Katy glanced at him. Was it her imagination or was he looking meaningly at Helen when he said that? She was certainly looking beautiful in a dress of clinging white jersey silk, one creamy shoulder bare and her blonde hair swept to one side in an elegant swirl, caught with a sparkling clip. Katy tore her eyes away and looked at Toby who was blinking sleepily.

'I think it's high time you said goodnight,' she told him. To her surprise he made no protest as she accompanied him up the stairs. When he was in bed she took the peak-flow meter and chart in to him, and to her concern she saw that the reading was alarmingly low. She glanced at the child. He was pale. All the zest and energy had fallen from him. Had she allowed him to do too much today, she wondered.

'Are you sleepy, Toby?' she asked. He nodded and snuggled down in his bed, clutching Arnold close.

As she came out on to the landing she met Claire coming upstairs. 'I was just coming to tell you that I'll stay up here close to Toby this evening,' she said, glad to have an excuse not to go down again. 'I think he may have overtired himself a little. He's asleep at the moment, but his PF reading was rather low.'

Claire smiled. 'Just as you feel best. You must be tired yourself. I'll say goodnight then if Toby has already dropped off.'

Katy closed her door. From downstairs came the sound of laughter and she felt like an outsider. Supposing—just supposing, she speculated, she had not called a halt last night. What would the situation be now? But her mind refused to supply the answer. Surely he must be glad not to have entangled himself—especially now that he had met this fabulous creature. How could she ever have imagined that Sean could feel as she did? At best their affair would have been brief and—for her—poignant. Perhaps she had escaped a worse hurt than she felt now.

She woke to a cry and sat up, instantly alert, to glance at the bedside clock. It was two am. Sliding out of bed she pulled on her dressing-down and ran into the next room. Toby was sitting up in bed, leaning forward, his face flushed, his shoulders heaving with the effort of breathing. Rapidly she took pillows from the cupboard and piled them into the chair by the bed, then she lifted Toby into it and propped him upright with the pillows. She took his inhaler from the drawer and held it to his lips, noticing with a surge of pity the sucked-in muscles around his neck and the white line encircling his mouth. Reassuringly she patted his cheek.

'Try to relax, darling, and breathe your inhaler. Katy's here—' She bent to pick up the battered teddy from the floor where it had fallen. 'Here—cuddle Arnold, he'll help make you better.' Toby managed a feeble smile and drew in the healing vapour of the inhaler that would help to dilate his closed bronchial tubes. After a few breaths he grew visibly better, his colour improved and he began to relax.

'The fish—' he mumbled as his breath returned. 'It was the fish.'

Katy shook her head. 'What do you mean, darling—the fish we had for dinner?'

He shook his head. 'I dreamed about a fish. It was looking at me with those funny eyes—it was alive and—and—swimming around inside my chest so that I couldn't breathe.'

Katy hugged him. 'There—it's all over now. You don't have to worry about it any more. Let's get you back into bed, shall we?'

Tucked back into bed, slightly propped up by extra pillows, Toby looked much better and Katy smiled at him. 'Try to get back to sleep. I'll leave my door open in case you need me again, but I'm sure you won't.'

'It won't come back if I go to sleep again, will it?' he asked anxiously. She shook her head firmly.

'No, Toby. It won't come back—I promise.'

Back in her own bed she thought about it. Why had Toby dreamed about the fish? And what had been so disturbing about it that it brought on an asthma attack? It was something she must write down in her report and discuss with Sean when she saw him next.

At breakfast the following morning Helen announced that she was off to Raikeside Lodge for the day.

'Sean was telling me about the thesis he's writing and he seems to be getting into rather a muddle with his notes,' she explained. 'I offered to go and do a little secretarial work for him this morning and in return he's going to show me some of the local scenery this afternoon.'

Jake looked up from his morning paper. 'Well I like that! Here's me gasping for a good secretary and you're off to help Sean! A fine girlfriend you turned out to be!'

Helen laughed. 'You have a wife—Sean

124

hasn't. You should have married me instead of Claire. You can't have everything in this life, my lad.'

'Ah—that's the way of it, is it?' Jake said with a twinkle. 'Sean is *available*! I wondered what a highly-paid magazine editor was doing pounding a typewriter—now I understand!'

Claire looked shocked. 'Jake! Really!' But Helen laughed good-naturedly.

'It's a good job I know and love you so well, Jake Underwood,' she told him. 'If I didn't, I might think you were one of the worst male chauvinists I'd ever met!'

Katy listened to all this good-natured banter thoughtfully, wondering if there could be any truth in what Jake said. Was the typing really an excuse for them to spend a day together? Sean certainly hadn't wasted any time, she told herself bitterly.

Jake threw down his paper and walked to the window. 'I'm having the day off!' he announced suddenly. 'Last night I reached the halfway mark in my book and I think I've earned a treat.' He turned to face them. 'How about it, Toby—shall we go exploring?'

Toby's little face lit up. 'Ooh, yes please, Daddy.' He turned to Claire. 'Are you coming too?'

She shook her head, smiling. 'No. Today is just for you and Daddy. When we took this house for the summer I promised to keep the garden in good order so this will be a good opportunity to get down to it.' She looked at Katy who was wondering where she fitted into the day's plans. 'Would you like to give me a hand, Katy? Does gardening appeal to you? We could have our lunch out there if the weather stays fine.'

'I'd love that,' Katy told her. 'I was brought up to help with the gardening and I've really missed it since I left home.'

The house seemed quiet after the others had left—Helen for Raikeside Lodge in her elegant sports car, and Toby and Jake in the family saloon, complete with picnic basket, heading for a certain celebrated ghyll with a hidden waterfall.

Claire heaved a sigh and looked at Katy with a smile. 'What do you say we have a coffee first,' she said. 'We'll have it on the terrace where it's nice and quiet and we can have a good chat.'

Over the coffee Katy told her about the attack Toby had suffered during the night and mentioned the dream about the fish. Claire shook her head.

'We've thought of all sorts of things that might trigger these attacks. You know, at one time I was convinced that the sound of the piano upset him.'

'Why should that be, do you think?' Katy asked.

'Didn't Sean tell you that Monique, Toby's mother, was a concert pianist? I'm afraid she

126

was rather a neurotic woman and when Toby was three she started to try and teach him to play. He didn't come up to her high ideals and I'm afraid she gave him rather a bad time of it.'

Katy was thoughtful. 'Three—that would be about the time he first contracted his asthma.'

'Exactly. Of course all that was a long time ago—long before Jake and I met and he doesn't like talking about it very much. But he did once tell me a little about the rages Monique used to fly into. Luckily Toby seems to have forgotten all about it now. Monique was killed in a plane crash when he was five and it was almost as though he blocked her out of his memory from that day. It's often the way, I believe—when something is too painful to remember and cope with, the mind simply blacks it out, but from what I've been reading on the subject, the subconscious has a nasty way of throwing up these forgotten memories when one least expects it.'

Katy was silent for a moment as she studied Claire's face. Did she know her well enough to say what was in her mind? She decided to risk it. 'When Sean told me about Toby's asthma returning after you and his father married I did wonder whether having a stepmother might be the cause,' she said. 'I'm just about to acquire a stepmother myself and

127

even at my age it can be traumatic.' She glanced quickly at Claire. 'Though of course I can see for myself that Toby has accepted you very lovingly.'

Claire sighed. 'I only wish it were something as simple as that.'

Katy enjoyed working in the garden. She had always found it restful and therapeutic, working in the open with plants and getting gloriously grubby with what her father called 'honest dirt'. As she worked she wondered where Sean and Helen were and what they were doing. Later, as they refreshed themselves with a pot of tea brought out to them by Mrs Benson, Claire voiced thoughts on the same subject.

'I'm glad Sean and Helen seem to be hitting it off so well. She's a lovely person, don't you think?'

Katy felt her cheeks colour and she bent to brush some imaginary dirt from her jeans, afraid that Claire might see and guess the reason. 'Yes,' she muttered. 'She's very smart and sophisticated.'

Claire laughed. 'I know what you mean. She always makes me feel like a frump! But of course she's always off to Paris and Rome—viewing the latest collections. I'm only surprised that she hasn't married before this, but she seems dedicated to her career. I don't mind admitting that when I saw her and Sean together last night I—' she broke off, looking closely at Katy. 'But there—I suppose because I'm so happily married I'm turning into a matchmaking old busybody.'

Katy bit her lip hard. Had Claire guessed the way she felt? She was hopeless at hiding her feelings—especially those she had for Sean. Not for the first time she cursed her colouring. Why did she have the kind of complexion that blushed in this awful tell-tale way?

Jake and Toby had still not returned by half past five and Katy thought she would walk down to the gates to meet them before going up to shower and change. It was cool among the trees and as she walked she suddenly glimpsed what she thought to be late violets growing in the peaty shade of the rhododendron bushes. She ducked under the low branches to look closer and as she did so she heard a car come round the curve of the drive and draw up close to where she stood, hidden by the shrubs. Thinking that it would be Jake and Toby she began to step forward, then she heard Sean's voice.

'I'll drop you off here if you don't mind, Helen. If Claire sees me she'll expect me to stay and I really must do some work this evening. I'll see that the wheel is changed for you and bring your car back tomorrow.'

'Thank you, Sean. It's very good of you.' It was Helen's voice. 'You must get a mechanic on to it and send me the bill. I can't have you

129

doing it yourself.'

Sean laughed. 'It's nothing—won't take me more than ten minutes. It's the least I can do for you after the help you've given me today.'

'Nonsense, I enjoyed every minute. I think this project of yours is fascinating. If you need any more help while I'm here, just let me know.'

'I will,' Sean assured her enthusiastically. 'I feel terrible, you know. I promised to show you the local scenery and we've done nothing but work all day. Look, will you let me take you out to dinner tomorrow night to make up.'

'There's no need—really.'

'I rarely ask a girl out because there's a *need*—not that kind anyway.'

Katy could imagine the expression on his face as he said it—cool and amused. But the sophisticated Helen wouldn't be floored by it! Her leg ached with standing still and she transferred her weight to the other foot. A twig snapped under her shoe. There was a pause, then she heard Sean say,

'Wait a minute—I do believe that little monkey Toby is hiding in the bushes. I'll teach him!' And before she could do anything the branches were parted and she found herself looking into his surprised face. 'Katy! What on earth are you doing hiding in the bushes?'

As she stared speechlessly at him she heard

Helen call: 'Thanks for bringing me home, Sean. I'll see you tomorrow.'

As her footsteps retreated Katy stood staring at Sean, her cheeks scarlet and her mouth open. He repeated his question.

'Why are you skulking in there?'

'I am not *skulking!*' she said between clenched teeth. 'I'm not hiding either. I just happened to come in here because I thought I saw some violets. I didn't *want* to listen to your attempts at—at—wooing!'

He looked at her coolly. 'I see—violets, is it?' He looked her up and down. 'What on earth have you been doing with yourself—you're covered in dirt—or are they freckles?'

Anguished, she rubbed at her nose with the back of one grimy hand. 'I'm not, am I?'

He burst out laughing. 'Now I can see that they're freckles—and you've just added a rather fetching smudge to go with them! Don't tell me gardening is another of your talents.'

She looked up at him. 'I can type too,' she told him. 'If you'd asked me I would have helped you type your notes—' She broke off as he looked intently at her, the smile fading from his face.

'You have enough to do, Katy,' he said quietly. 'I wouldn't have presumed on your free time.'

She turned away, misery eating at her

131

heart, but he caught her wrist and held her.

'Katy—what is it? You're not—jealous of Helen, are you?'

Her temper saved her. Her green eyes blazed at him, scorching him with their fire. 'Jealous? Why should I be jealous—because of the attention *you're* paying her, I suppose! As if *I* care who you take out. Your—your—philandering doesn't affect me in the least. I could see the sort you were right from the first—that's why I decided not to have anything to do with you.'

He stared at her for a moment. Then he burst out laughing. 'Katy—you're priceless! Where do you get all these antique words from? *Wooing—philandering*—you make me feel like a character from Shakespeare!'

'Huh! *Romeo*, no doubt! And I'm glad you think it's funny.'

'Well it is. You must admit it. Here we are arguing in the bushes with you all covered in dirt and freckles.' He took both her wrists and pulled her towards him. 'And what do you mean—you decided to have nothing to do with me? That wasn't the impression I got when—Ow!' His hand flew to his cheek as she pulled one hand away to deal him a ringing slap. 'Ow—you little—'

But Katy fled, stumbling through the bushes and back towards the house. Her anger and humiliation would be contained no longer and she was determined not to let him see their effect.

## CHAPTER NINE

Helen showed no sign of wanting to go home to London and Claire was obviously glad to have her company. It seemed that she had four weeks' leave from her job and had spent only a week of it in Scotland. Sean took her out on several occasions and she went to Raikeside Lodge to help him with his work twice more. On the evenings he came to dinner at Bridge House Katy kept out of his way as much as possible, and one evening when Claire came up to say goodnight to Toby she mentioned this.

'Katy—there's nothing wrong between you and Sean is there?'

Katy shook her head. 'Nothing at all.'

Claire sat down on her bed. 'I'm sorry, but I'm afraid I can't quite believe that my dear. When he's here you and he hardly speak. I just thought there might be something I could do to put it right.'

Katy winced inwardly. 'No—as a matter of fact we had a—disagreement and I lost my temper. It was stupid and unforgivable. I suppose I shall have to apologise. I'm sorry if it's made an atmosphere,' she concluded miserably, sinking on to the dressing-table

133

stool.

Claire looked at her closely, frowning. Suddenly she put out her hand and touched Katy's arm. 'Oh dear—you're in love with him, aren't you? I was afraid that might happen.' She shook her head in exasperation. 'Damn the man! He seems totally oblivious to the effect he has on young, vulnerable girls like you. It's all right for people like Helen—she can cope.' She pressed Katy's hand. 'Is there anything—anything at all—I can do to help, love?'

'Nothing at all,' Katy said bleakly. 'And don't worry, I shall cope in my own way—I certainly shan't go running off or anything silly like that.' She didn't add that she had nowhere to run to, or that unhappy or not she still preferred to be in Sean's company rather than out of it. 'Anyway, he's far too old for me—positively *middle-aged*, really!'

Claire laughed. 'Watch it, girl! Sean is two years younger than me, I'll have you know.' Then, seeing Katy's confusion, she added, 'Not that I don't feel middle-aged at times.' She reached out to pat Katy's shoulder. 'Anyway, I'm relieved to hear that you don't have plans for running off. I know it would break Toby's heart to lose you now.'

Since Toby's attack on the night of Helen's arrival Toby had not had another. Katy had scrupulously recorded anything she thought might be of significance in the diary and

134

continued the peak-flow chart, night and morning. But over the past two days another problem had cropped up: Toby had complained several times about toothache and when she had looked into his mouth she had discovered that one of his temporary molars had a large cavity. She mentioned it to Claire.

'It seems to be causing him quite a bit of discomfort and it looks to me as though there was once a filling there that has dropped out.'

Claire nodded. 'The dentist at home was keeping an eye on that one. Maybe we should pay a visit to a dentist here. I'll ask Mrs Benson if she knows a nice kind one.'

An appointment was made for Toby for that afternoon, much to his disgust, and Claire said that she would drive him and Katy into Harrogate, promising Toby a treat afterwards. They set off after an early lunch, arriving in good time, and were shown the waiting-room by a brisk receptionist. Unlike many waiting-rooms that Katy knew, it was tastefully furnished in bright colours. On three of the walls were cheerful prints and on the other was an aquarium with colourful tropical fish swimming in and out of waving vegetation. The whole thing was illuminated with concealed lighting and as soon as Claire saw it she exclaimed with delight.

'Oh look! What a good idea. Just the thing for a dentist's waiting-room. Look Toby.'

Toby *was* looking. Fascinated by the pretty

135

little creatures, he stood staring at them almost as though hypnotised while Claire and Katy sat down with selected magazines from the pile on the table in the centre of the room.

'This month's *Vogue!*' Claire exclaimed. 'This is a dentist after my own heart!'

There was only one other patient in the room and presently the receptionist came in to escort him to the surgery. A moment later a sound made Katy look up. Toby was wheezing. He began to cough, going into a paroxysm, his little face red and distressed, his shoulders heaving. Katy scrabbled in her handbag for his inhaler, but this time it seemed to have little effect. Claire stood looking anxiously on.

'What on earth can have brought it on?' she asked. 'He's never been that worried about a visit to the dentist before. Isn't there anything I can do, Katy?'

Katy looked up at her. 'A glass of water might help.' Above Toby's head she mouthed, 'Ring Sean!'

The dentist's brisk receptionist acted with great presence of mind and moments later, as they waited for Sean to arrive, Toby was receiving oxygen administered by the dentist in his surgery. At last the attack abated and by the time Sean actually arrived they were all drinking tea while they tried to recover from the shock. As usual Toby was completely himself the moment the attack was over and

136

persisted in reminding Claire that she had promised him a treat. Sean looked at Claire. 'You take him, he'll be all right now. I'll take Katy home.' His tone was firm and with a sinking heart Katy guessed that he would use the opportunity to talk to her. As she got into his car her knees shook. He drove out of the car park and on to the road, silent as he waited for the lights to change then manoeuvred into the correct lane. When they were safely on their way he looked at her.

'You've been avoiding me.'

She shook her head. 'You knew where I was if you wanted—wanted to discuss anything with me.'

'That's not what I mean and you know it.'

She didn't answer but looked straight ahead through the windscreen.

'Katy,' he said, 'I'm not playing some silly game with you. I want to talk—about Toby. I'd like to see your reports and the peak-flow chart—also to hear your observations, if you've got any.'

'Of course,' she said stiffly.

He glanced at her. 'It was you who stressed the professional character of this job, Katy. It isn't fair to Toby to let personal feelings get in the way.'

She turned a pair of flashing eyes on him. 'Who's doing *that*? I'm certainly not!'

'But you are,' he insisted calmly. 'You're angry with me. Oh, I know I teased you the other day. I'm sorry if you were unduly upset by it. I had no idea I could provoke such a violent reaction.' He fingered his left cheek reminiscently. 'By the way, that's a vicious right hook you've got.' He grinned wryly and she averted her eyes.

'It was pure impulse. I let myself down. I'm sorry.'

'Right—we're all square then. Friends again?'

His smile melted her heart but she couldn't resist asking, 'Didn't you bring Helen with you?'

He looked surprised. 'Why should I? She doesn't spend all her time with me, you know.' He glanced at her. 'She really has been a marvellous help to me. She's good company too, I'm sure you'll agree.'

'I expect you have your own ideas about "good company",' she said dryly. Sean's mouth set in a grim line as he realised the implication behind her words as she had meant them and he didn't say another word to her as they drove towards Belldon Cross. Katy sank unhappily into her seat. Why *couldn't* she curb this acid tongue of hers?

Helen's car was parked outside when they arrived at Bridge House and they found her having tea with Jake on the terrace. He was delighted to see Sean and invited him and Katy to join them.

'Katy and I have a little work to attend to

138

first,' Sean said determinedly. 'But we'll be with you in a moment.' Taking her arm he propelled her firmly up the stairs to Toby's room and she fetched her notebook and the peak-flow chart. For a few minutes all their differences were forgotten as they studied them together. Sean shook his head.

'This morning's output was normal according to this—so what triggered off the attack in the dentist's waiting-room?'

'The obvious answer would be fear or anxiety,' Katy said. 'But I doubt that very much in Toby's case. It's certainly very puzzling.'

'Can you swim?' Sean asked her suddenly.

'Swim? Yes, pretty well as it happens—why?'

'I think it might be a good idea for Toby to learn. The exercise would help expand his chest. Lots of kids with respiratory complaints benefit. The weather is warm enough now. Start him off at the baths, then later you could swim in the river here. It's quite safe and not at all polluted.'

She nodded. 'All right. I'll see how the idea appeals to him.'

He looked thoughtful. 'If all else fails I do have one last resort. I have a friend in York—we qualified together—he works a lot with hypnotherapy.' He pulled a wry face at her. 'I have to admit that so far I've been sceptical about his theories but now I'm beginning to wonder.' He looked down at the diary Katy had been keeping. 'I wonder if these dreams of his have any significance.'

She shrugged. 'We all dream oddly at times. It may not mean anything more than an over-active mind. But I thought I'd better put everything down.'

He nodded, smiling at her. 'You're doing a very good job Katy, as I knew you would—and Toby obviously adores you.'

'He's a very lovable child.' She got up and walked to the door. Sean followed her out on to the landing and put a hand on her shoulder.

'Katy—look at me a minute.'

It was the one thing she couldn't trust herself to do. Looking into those dark eyes she felt sure that she would give her feelings away—betray the hopeless longing in her heart.

'We—should be getting back to the others,' she said evasively.

'There's no hurry.' His hand was still on her shoulder and he turned her firmly towards him. 'What *is* it you're so angry with me over?' he asked, looking searchingly into her eyes. 'Surely it isn't Helen? After all, you've made your own feelings abundantly clear.'

She forced a laugh. 'I haven't the slightest idea what you're talking about—what feelings? I'm not aware that I have any

140

feelings on that score. Why on earth should I care one way or the other who you take out?'

She moved to break away but he grasped both her shoulders and held her firmly. His eyes were angry now as he looked down at her. 'I'll show you why, you little idiot!' His mouth came down hard on hers, taking her breath away. For a moment she resisted, holding herself stiffly, then as his arms slid round her to draw her close, she began to relax. She closed her eyes, feeling as though she were melting into him—growing weak with love—then suddenly a voice from somewhere below startled her.

'Are you still up there, you two? Mrs Benson has just made a fresh pot of tea. If you don't come and drink it soon it'll be cold!'

Katy pushed Sean from her and took a step backwards, blushing crimson as she caught sight of Helen who had just reached the top of the stairs. She paused uncertainly, looking from one to the other.

'Oh—I'm sorry—I—'

'We were just coming down, weren't we, Katy?' Sean said breezily, striding ahead of her down the staircase.

Helen followed with a brief glance behind her at Katy. 'How is your work going?' she asked on the way down. 'I shall be going back to London in a couple of days, so I don't suppose we shall be seeing each other again.'

He laughed. 'Good Lord! London isn't the other side of the world. Surely we don't have to say goodbye for ever! You must let me have your phone number. I'll ring you when I'm in Town and we can have dinner.' At the bottom of the stairs he glanced at Katy but she returned his look defiantly, chin up.

Inside she was still trembling from his kiss. How could he be so cruel—playing this cat and mouse game? Why did he enjoy hurting her so much?

*　　*　　*

Toby had his first swimming lesson the very next day. Claire had been doubtful about it but Katy had assured her that the whole thing was Sean's idea and perfectly safe.

'The exercise and controlled breathing will be extremely good for his lungs,' she explained. 'And the achievement will help him too. Asthmatic children often feel inadequate and it's important that he learns to compete with other boys of his age.'

He did well, eager to learn and taking great pleasure from the water, and when Katy told him that as soon as he could swim confidently out of his depth she would take him swimming in the river at Bridge House, he was even more eager to become proficient.

When they arrived home that afternoon Claire, Jake and Helen were having tea together and the air was charged with excitement as they discussed a telephone call Jake had just received from his agent. His American publisher was in England and planned to visit Jake with a view to his making a promotion tour of the States. As the conversation buzzed excitedly back and forth Katy sensed Helen was looking at her thoughtfully.

When at last Jake got up to return to his study Claire rose too.

'I'd better go and break the news to Mrs Benson that we shall be entertaining this weekend.' She laughed. 'It looks as though she'll be needing her faithful *Mrs Beeton* again!' Toby ran after her, frustrated that his new achievement had been overshadowed.

'Wait for me! I want to tell Mrs Benson about how I can nearly swim!'

Helen laughed. 'Poor Toby. I'm afraid his guns have been well and truly spiked this afternoon.'

Although Katy had felt pangs of envy over Helen she could not deny that she was a pleasant person. Throughout her stay she had shown nothing but kindness and friendliness to her—but still she got the feeling that there was something she was trying to say—something she was finding difficult.

'Katy,' she ventured after a moment. 'Forgive me if I'm wrong, but I have the feeling that somehow or other I've trodden on your toes.'

Katy felt her cheeks burning. 'Of course you haven't. How could you possibly have done that?' she protested.

Helen smiled gently. 'Only you can know that. The point is, I shall be going in a couple of days and I'd like to make amends in some way. It occurs to me that you might be thinking of getting a new dress for this dinner party at the weekend. Perhaps you'd let me help you choose it?'

Katy stiffened. Was Helen implying tactfully that she looked a shambles and might let Jake and Claire down? Helen read her thoughts.

'Oh—please don't be offended,' she said quickly. 'You always look charming—but you do have a greater potential. I hope that, as a fashion expert, I can help you realise it.'

Katy swallowed her hurt pride. Looking at the sincerity in Helen's eyes she knew that it was meant kindly—also that it was an offer definitely not to be passed up. She had to admit that she would give a lot to look as elegant as Helen. She smiled.

'That would be marvellous, if you're sure you can spare the time—oh—and as long as it won't cost a fortune.'

Helen laughed. 'It needn't at all. With your looks and youth—and that fantastic colouring, simplicity is the order of the day.'

Obviously Helen saw the project in terms

of her daily work and Katy began to feel privileged. 'But giving up the last day of your holiday—you'll be back at work soon enough.' But Helen waved her protests aside.

'I'll ask Claire if Toby can do without you for one day and we'll go into Harrogate tomorrow. Is it a date?'

As they drove into town the following morning Katy couldn't help noticing that Helen kept shooting glances at her. At last she voiced what was on her mind.

'Have you ever considered trying another hairstyle?'

Katy looked at her in surprise. 'Not really. It's so unruly that there isn't much I can do with it. It refuses to lie flat in today's smooth styles.'

Helen nodded sympathetically. 'I'm not a hair expert but a marvellous stylist we often use on the magazine lives up here in Harrogate. He's semi-retired now, though he still has a salon in London—' she glanced at Katy. 'As a matter of fact I rang him last night and said we might be looking in on him—but of course it's entirely up to you.'

Katy looked at her, thinking of the constant struggle she had in keeping her long auburn tresses tidy. 'All right,' she said impulsively. 'I'll do it!'

Helen's hairdresser friend, Aubrey, was a tall, willowy man of about fifty. He lived in an elegant little Georgian town house and he answered the door to Helen's ring himself, clasping her warmly and kissing her on both cheeks.

'Helen darling. How marvellous to see you. Do come in, both of you.' As he closed the door he took a look at Katy's hair and raised his hands in horror. 'Heavens! What a shame! High time someone took it in hand, dear.' He looked at Helen. 'How wise of you to bring her to me and not let some of these scissor cowboys loose on it!'

In his tiny salon at the back of the house he pushed Katy into a chair and began to study her hair and face in the mirror. His fingers under her chin, he twisted her head this way and that, then turned to Helen.

'*Criminal* to hide bone structure like this. So gamine—positively elfin. At the moment she looks as though she's peering through a bush! It must all come off, of course.'

Katy started up in alarm. 'All off—but—'

'Do sit still, dear,' Aubrey said tetchily, pushing her back into the chair. He enveloped her in a large overall. 'Shampoo first,' he said gleefully. 'Oh, you'll be *amazed* at the difference I shall make to you!'

Katy sank back with an air of resignation. She was prepared to believe him!

One hour later she sat staring at her reflection in the mirror, stunned into silence. Looking back at her was a small oval face with huge green eyes, made to look even

146

larger by the smooth, shining cap of hair Aubrey had created. He had cut it with the curl rather than against it and it lay over her ears and forehead in one continuous swirl of gleaming red-gold. Helen viewed it with beaming admiration.

'Aubrey, you're a genius!'

He stood back, admiring his handiwork. 'Well of course I am, darling. Haven't I always told you so?'

She laughed. 'Modest to a fault as usual. What do you think, Katy?'

Katy was still reeling from the shock. 'Well—it's certainly a change.'

Aubrey gave it a final flick with the comb, peering at her through the mirror with half closed eyes. 'If I might venture to suggest just a *soupçon* more eye make-up, sweetie—and perhaps a brighter shade of lipstick?' He sighed with satisfaction at his own handiwork. 'You'll have every head in the street turning.'

Outside Katy felt self-conscious. Aubrey had been right—she *did* feel that people were looking at her—and she wasn't sure that she liked the experience. Helen chose a small exclusive boutique in a quiet little side street and, once inside, she combed the rails with concentration, picking out a dress here and there and holding it against Katy thoughtfully. None of them was remotely the kind of thing Katy would have chosen had she been alone, though she had to admit that one or two of them were quite stunning.

'I don't want anything too conspicuous,' she whispered. Helen stared at her, one eyebrow raised. 'Well—I've always felt that my hair made me stand out quite enough,' she explained.

'My dear girl, you play up your best features—don't try to submerge them!' Helen threw half a dozen dresses over her arm. 'These will do for a start,' she said. 'Come on, let's see how they look.'

They both agreed that the most effective dress was the first one she tried—a slim fitting gown in a vibrant shade of sea-green.

'It makes your skin look like ivory and your eyes like turquoise,' Helen said poetically. 'I'm beginning to think I should take you back to London with me to be photographed for the magazine!'

Back at Bridge House the 'new' Katy met with a mixed reception. Jake and Claire were vehemently approving but Toby had reservations. For a long time he stood staring at her, his head on one side.

'You've had all your hair cut off,' he said at last, pouting. 'I liked it better as it was before—all sort of fluffy. Will it take long for it to grow again?'

★    ★    ★

The arrangements for Saturday's dinner party went smoothly. Claire did her best to persuade Helen to stay but she was adamant.

'I have a designer to see first thing on Monday morning,' she said. 'And I lent my flat to a friend for the month—heaven knows what state it will be in by now. Thanks, Claire, but I have a million things to do.'

So, on Friday afternoon they waved her goodbye as she drove down the drive in her gleaming sports car for the last time. Before she went she gave Katy a warm hug.

'Give me a ring at the office whenever you come up to London and we'll have lunch,' she said. 'And just stop underestimating yourself,' she added in a whisper. 'Good luck, love.'

Katy watched her go wistfully, wishing that they had had more time to get to know one another.

Toby was impatient for his second swimming lesson so Katy took him to the swimming pool again that afternoon. He took to the water gleefully and by the time he came home he had taken his first unaided stroke. His excitement knew no bounds and he could hardly wait to get home and tell everyone of his triumph.

'And Katy said that when I could swim properly we could swim here in the river,' he said happily. 'When can we, Katy—tomorrow?'

149

She laughed as she shook her head. 'Heavens, no! I *said* when you can swim confidently out of your own depth. You've a little way to go yet.'

But Toby was not to be put off. 'Well, I bet I could if I tried. Oh, *do* let me try, Katy,' he begged. 'You'll be there—you wouldn't let me drown.'

'Well, we'll have to see,' she told him. 'Anyway it will have to be after the weekend now—when Daddy's special guests have gone.'

As Saturday drew near Katy was beginning to have grave doubts about the dinner party. Did she have any place at such an occasion? Helen had taken it for granted that she was to be there but perhaps Jake and Claire would prefer it if she ate in her room instead. She voiced these thoughts to Claire who was outraged at such an idea.

'But of course you must be there! Why, you've bought a new dress and had your hair done specially. Besides, you'll make the numbers right.' Katy looked puzzled and she went on, 'There'll be Jake and I, Jake's agent and the editor from America—Dave Maskell, Sean and you. Oh—perhaps you hadn't realised that Lesley Francis, Jake's agent, was a woman!' She laughed. 'I'm relying on you and Sean to keep the others off "shop" all evening!'

Katy was slightly comforted, although the

thought of competing conversationally with all those brilliant people still daunted her a little. Claire laughed at her fears.

'Just be your charming self, my dear, and you can't go wrong, I promise you!'

The two guests of honour arrived just after lunch on Saturday and for the rest of the afternoon they were in conference with Jake in his study, discussing plans for the coming tour. Katy took Toby for another swimming lesson at the pool and to the cinema afterwards for a special treat, with tea afterwards as he wouldn't be joining the grown-ups for dinner that evening. He was tired when they got back to Bridge House and quite ready for bed, but he made Katy promise that she would come and show herself to him when she was ready to go down.

She took a leisurely bath and dressed carefully, making up her face as Helen had shown her, using the cool green eyeshadow and complementing the vibrant colour of the dress with a warm, coral pink lipstick. When she stood back to assess the result she had to admit that it was startlingly different from her former appearance. A smooth, sculptured look replaced the flyaway mop of hair and the dark green clinging material of the dress accentuated the curves of her figure seductively; finally, the new make-up gave her the look of sophistication she had always envied. Deep inside she felt a warm tingle of anticipation. Picking up her evening bag of toning green and silver she tiptoed into Toby's room but found him already fast asleep, clutching Arnold. Maybe it was just as well, she told herself wryly. With one phrase Toby was capable of shattering the most inspired illusion!

Jake and Claire were entertaining their guests to cocktails in the drawing-room and she stood hesitantly in the doorway until Jake noticed her and came across to take her arm and draw her into the room.

'This is our good friend, Katy Lang, who is doing such a marvellous job with my young son, Toby,' he said as he led her forward. 'Katy, this is my agent, Miss Lesley Francis, and this is Dave Maskell from New York—he is my editor from Globe Publishing.'

The tall, good-looking American smiled at her with candid admiration as he took her hand. 'Well, well! This is certainly my idea of what a nurse should be. Lucky old Toby! I don't know where you found her Jake, but I feel good just looking at her!'

Katy blushed under his frank appraisal and was grateful when the doorbell rang and Claire beckoned to her.

'Katy—that will be Sean. Will you answer the door to him? Mrs Benson is doing something vital with the soufflé and I told her to ignore everything else.'

Katy was glad of the chance to escape. As she passed the hall mirror she took a look at herself and tugged at a wisp of hair, wishing that her heart would stop leaping about so disconcertingly in her chest.

She took a deep breath and opened the door. Sean looked very handsome in evening dress. He stepped inside then stopped dead, staring at her, his eyes sweeping over her from head to foot and back again.

'Katy—Oh, my God! What on earth have you done to yourself?'

Her face was frozen into immobility and she held out her hand wordlessly for his coat. Claire came out into the hall to see what was holding them up.

'What's the matter with you, Sean? You look as though you'd just seen a ghost.' She looked from one to the other.

Sean pointed to Katy. 'Was this your idea?'

Claire looked furious as she said, 'Sean! For heaven's sake! Katy looks perfectly charming. She's already been receiving the most glowing compliments from our American guests.'

Sean gave a bark of derision. 'Huh! I suppose that makes it all right then,' he said sarcastically.

'Listen, Sean, this evening is important to Jake. I hope you're not going to spoil it!' Claire took Katy's arm, flashing Sean a searing look. 'Come back into the drawing-room. Perhaps Sean will join us when he has recovered. If I didn't know you better Sean I'd suspect that you'd been drinking!'

Katy turned away, her cheeks pink and her eyes bright with the hurt she was unable to hide. Sean hadn't been drinking—far from it. He couldn't have been more sober. Obviously to him she looked like a little girl, dressed up in grown-up clothes. So much for her attempt at sophistication!

The dinner party was a resounding success. The meal was delicious, the conversation sparkling and—on the surface at least—everyone seemed to be in good spirits. For Katy it was a total failure, though she didn't allow her feelings to show. Claire had placed her next to the American, Dave Maskell, who flirted shamelessly with her throughout the meal. Opposite sat Sean, next to Lesley Francis, with whom he seemed to have a great deal in common—she had a brother who was a doctor. Their conversation sounded fascinating to Katy but she was not included. Cornered by Jake's guest of honour she forced herself to keep up a steady flow of small talk. Obviously he thought her as empty-headed as Sean did.

After coffee Claire invited them all into the drawing-room again. Soft music was playing and the french windows were open on to the terrace. The minute she could, Katy excused herself and went outside, breathing in the cool evening air gratefully and wishing that the ordeal could be over as soon as possible. It occurred to her fleetingly that Helen had known what Sean's reaction would be and had encouraged her to change her appearance purposely. But she tossed the thought aside as unworthy, sure that Helen had acted out of generosity and nothing else. She wandered down to the water's edge and was watching the smoothly flowing stream when a voice behind her made her start.

'Katy—forgive me. I behaved atrociously.'

She turned to see Sean standing behind her and her heart gave the familiar painful lurch. Suddenly she was angry—both with him and with herself. Why did she allow him to have this power over her? Why was it that no matter how he treated her she was ready to forget it the moment he smiled?

'Yes, you did behave badly,' she told him. 'And if it was your intention to spoil my evening you can congratulate yourself that you almost succeeded—*almost*, but not quite. From now on I intend to enjoy myself.'

A frown replaced his smile. 'Indeed? You seemed to me to be enjoying yourself at dinner—quite a lot, in fact.'

She stared at him. 'I wasn't aware that you were interested in whether I was enjoying myself or not!'

He laughed shortly. 'One could hardly miss

the abandoned way you were flirting with that American,' he said heatedly.

'I was doing nothing of the kind,' Katy retorted. 'Anyway, what right do you have to criticise me, when for the past fortnight you've been throwing yourself at Helen Kent's feet?'

He smiled sardonically. 'Ah—so that's it, is it? Now we're getting to it. You thought you'd try to play me at my own game—well let me tell you, Katy, that to do that you'd first have to understand how my mind works—and that you never will.'

'You flatter yourself!' she hissed at him, afraid that their rising voices would carry across the lawn to the ears of the others. 'Why should *I* care about the wonderful workings of your mind? Your thoughts—and the rest of you too—are of *supreme* indifference to me and I hope you'll remember it!' And with that she swung round and began to walk back towards the house. But as she passed him he grasped her by the wrist and held her fast, his face dark with anger.

'Don't you dare to speak to me like that,' he growled. 'It's time you remembered that it was me who recommended you for this job, that I am a doctor and you are a nurse—and a *failed* nurse at that!'

She gasped as though he had hit her and for a moment silence hung heavily between them.

'What I choose to do with my own life is

my affair, as I've told you before,' she told him quietly, the breath catching in her throat. 'I suppose you were also pulling rank when you expected me to let you make love to me?'

It was Sean's turn to be speechless. 'That was uncalled for,' he said at last. 'But I agree that it was a mistake—and it's one that won't be repeated, that I *can* promise you.' He glanced towards the house. 'Maybe you'd better get back to your American. He's old enough to be your father—but maybe that's what you're looking for!' He let go of her wrist abruptly and strode across the lawn.

Katy was beside herself with rage. If he hadn't stopped her she would have been the one to walk away. Now it was he who had had the last word. She stamped her foot in frustration, hot tears pricking her eyelids. Well he wouldn't get away with it! She'd show him he hadn't the power to punish her—she *really* would!

Back in the drawing-room she responded to Dave Maskell's flirting wholeheartedly. From time to time she glanced across the room to see if Sean was noticing but he never allowed himself the slightest look in her direction. As she laughed and joked with Dave, returning the pressure of his hand on hers, her eyes sparkled. Her row with Sean had made the adrenalin flow copiously and it was almost as though she were high on it. She enjoyed playing the part even while telling herself that

157

this time she and Sean had surely reached the point of no return. Tonight they had both said things that would not easily be forgotten.

It was well after midnight when Lesley Francis announced that she was ready for her bed and Claire fetched her coat and Dave's. They were staying at an hotel in Harrogate as there was no room for them at Bridge House. Jake and Claire walked out to their car with them. At the door Dave slipped an arm round Katy's waist and bent to kiss her lightly.

'Thank you for a very special evening, Katy,' he said softly. 'I hope that the next time I'm in England I can take you out to dinner.'

Katy smiled up at him. 'That would be very nice. It's been fun meeting you Dave. Goodnight.' She wandered back into the drawing-room to collect her bag and was startled to find Sean standing just inside the door, quivering with suppressed anger. Quite clearly he had seen and heard her exchange with Dave Maskell.

'Dressing up like that seems to have completely altered your personality,' he said coldly. 'I suppose you realise that you've behaved this evening like a little tramp. I hope you're proud of yourself!'

Outside, the roar of a car engine could be heard and shouted farewells. Katy stared at Sean, the only outward sign of the emotion raging inside her the rapid rise and fall of her

158

breast. Claire and Jake came laughing back into the room and Jake slipped a friendly arm about her waist.

'Well, you certainly made a big hit with Dave,' he said happily. 'Thank you for helping to make the evening a success, Katy love. I'm beginning to think I'd better take you to the States with me to act as my PRO!'

'And you look so lovely too,' Claire told her. 'Dave has just confided to me that you are the prettiest English girl he's met so far.'

Neither of them had noticed Sean leave the room but a moment later they heard the roar of his car engine as he took off at speed down the drive. Jake and Claire looked at each other.

'What's the matter with him tonight?' Jake asked. 'He's been in a strange mood all evening.' He looked at his wife. 'Do you think he's missing Helen? They did make a perfect couple, didn't they? Time old Sean got married. It'd settle him down.'

Claire shot him a warning look and took Katy by the arm. 'Let's go and have a look at Toby,' she said, frowning at Jake behind her back. 'It's been a long day for all of us. I expect you're as ready for your bed as I am.'

# CHAPTER TEN

'Watch me, Daddy—look, Claire!' Toby, looking small and vulnerable in his minute swimming trunks, ran across the grass to the edge of the bank. The stretch of river that ran through the garden of Bridge House was more than six feet deep in the middle, but the edges were shallow. Crystal clear water bubbled over smooth stones and Toby tested it with one toe.

'Ooh! It's cold.'

'I told you it was cooler than the pool water.' Katy was already in and waiting for him, up to her waist halfway to midstream. The cool water felt delicious as it swirled around her and she held out her hands to Toby.

'Come on, it's lovely when you're used to it. Get in and duck under like we did at the pool.'

He stepped gingerly in and began to kick at the water, sending up a spray of rainbow droplets and shouting with laughter. 'This is fun!' He stepped in further, till the water came up to his thighs, then reached out towards Katy's outstretched hands.

'That's right,' she encouraged. 'A little further, then start to swim to me.'

Toby splashed forward into the water and

struck out, arriving at where Katy stood in four strokes. She caught his hands and pulled him upright.

'Well done!'

Toby turned triumphantly towards Jake and Claire. 'Did you see me? I swam in the river—I'm almost out of my depth. Shall I swim some more?'

Claire looked anxiously at her husband. 'I wish he wouldn't. I can't really believe he's safe in there. What if he were swept away on a current or something?'

Jake shook his head. 'No problem. Katy's with him. She's a strong swimmer. She won't let him come to any harm.'

Leaving Toby standing in the shallows, Katy swam to the opposite bank and back. 'It's lovely!' she called. 'It's so clear that you can see the little fishes darting about. It took me fourteen strokes. You can do that, Toby. What about having a go?'

He looked at her hesitantly, wanting badly to try but just a little unsure. 'I—don't think I can,' he said, his teeth chattering a little.

'Yes you can, and you must keep moving or you'll get cold. I'll swim beside you and if you think you want to stop you can hang on to me.' She laughed and splashed him. 'Come on, chicken. Have a try!'

'All right.' He turned to Jake and Claire. 'Watch me. I'm going to swim all the way across there!'

Claire clutched at Jake's arm. 'I don't like it—I'm afraid.' But he only smiled.

'He'll be fine. He's quite a tough little chap really. You mustn't mollycoddle him. Katy knows what she's doing.'

To his great delight Toby made it to the other bank. When he reached it he stood waving his arms and shouting. 'I can *really* swim now. I swam the river!'

Katy laughed. She had been keeping a careful watch on him but there was no sign of breathlessness. 'Now, how about swimming back?' she asked. 'It's really the only way unless you want to walk up to the bridge and back. After you've done that I think we should get out and dry off.'

'Oh, no! We've only just got in and it's fun,' Toby protested. 'Uncle Sean said he'd come and watch me this afternoon and he isn't here yet. I want him to see me too.'

'There's plenty of time for that. Come on now, I don't want you to catch a cold.' Katy swam out a little way and turned towards him. 'Come on—this time you swim in front of me. You've done well and I'm very proud of you.'

Encouraged, he swam forward while Katy trod water, waiting for him to draw level with her.

It happened when he was at midstream. He turned to her suddenly, a look of panic on his face, then with an anguished cry he flung up

162

his arms and disappeared below the water's surface. Claire screamed and jumped up, running down to the water's edge. Katy reached Toby just as he was surfacing again and hooked an arm around his waist.

'It's all right, Toby, I've got you,' she gasped. 'Don't struggle, darling. I'll have you out in a moment.' But to her horror she soon realised the reason for his panic. He was wheezing painfully—having an attack!

Somehow she got him to the shallows and climbed out of the water with the child in her arms, helped by Jake. Claire threw a towel round the limp little body and snatched him from Katy.

'I knew something like this would happen!' she said, her voice shrill with fear. 'I said it was a stupid idea—letting him go in the river. You've nearly *killed* him you stupid girl!'

Jake took Toby from her and began to rub him dry. 'Pull yourself together Claire. It wasn't Katy's fault.'

'Please—' Katy begged, 'can we get him upstairs at once? I don't think you understand. He's having an asthma attack, not drowning!' She felt for the child's pulse and found it thin and thready. 'He may be going into shock too.' She looked anxiously at Jake, fear making her heart race. If only Sean were there, if only she were qualified—maybe Claire would have had more faith in her.

Suddenly there was the sound of a car door

163

slamming and Claire said,

'It's Sean—thank God!'

The half hour that followed was just a blur. Everything happened so fast. Sean scooped Toby up and indoors, and within minutes was administering oxygen with Katy's help. Slowly Toby recovered, opening his eyes to peer up at the anxious faces surrounding him.

'Where's Arnold?' he asked. Katy found the bear and pushed it into his arms. The wheezing was subsiding and he was breathing easier now.

'Toby, did something happen while you were swimming?' she asked. 'Did you get scared? You knew I was there, didn't you—right behind you?'

He looked at her for a long moment, then he said, 'It was a fish—a big one—just like the one in the dream.'

Sean took Katy's arm and drew her gently away from the bed. 'I'm going to give you an injection now, Toby,' he said. 'It might make you a bit sleepy, but don't worry, you won't dream.'

'You won't go away—you'll stay till I wake, won't you, Uncle Sean?'

Sean smiled reassuringly. 'Of course I will, old chap. I'll be waiting to play a game, eh?' A few moments later Toby's eyelids fluttered and closed.

Outside on the landing the four looked at each other. Sean shook his head.

'The trigger for his attacks gets to be more and more of a mystery. I do have one last resort and I'd like to talk to you about it in a little while. First, though, I want to have another look at the diary Katy has been keeping. I'll join you downstairs in a moment.'

Claire looked at Katy who was still wearing her wet swimsuit under a towelling robe. 'You really must have a hot bath, Katy, you'll catch cold.' She reached out to touch her hand. 'I'm sorry I shouted at you, dear. I was just so scared. It was as though I had a sort of premonition. I just *knew* something bad was going to happen. Toby looked so small and helpless. It wasn't your fault though. I know that now.'

Katy nodded. 'I was scared myself, I know how you must have felt. And you needn't worry—I shan't dare take him swimming again.'

Jake and Claire went downstairs and Sean followed her into her room.

'I'd like to look at the diary again,' he said. 'I can't help feeling that there's something we must have missed. It's strange that the pool didn't affect him, yet the river did.'

'The pool doesn't have fish,' Katy said. 'I don't know why but fish seem to panic him into an attack—first there was the night we had the salmon that Helen brought, then the tropical fish at the dentist's—now this. He said he saw a fish in the water.'

Sean nodded slowly. 'That's right—yet how and why does it affect him?' He was silent for a while, then he said, 'This is all the more reason why I think we should see John Marquand, the friend I told you about. He uses hypnotherapy and he's had some quite remarkable results. I'm not saying that it works in every case, but in Toby's I believe it's worth a try.'

'Won't he find it bewildering—how will you explain it to him? He's too intelligent to fob off with some fairy tale.'

Sean smiled. 'You're underestimating John. There's nothing bewildering about his methods and he has a small son of about Toby's age. I'll ring him and have a talk. I'm sure he'll come up with something.' He leafed through the diary. 'I see that at one stage you thought that Claire's piano playing brought on an attack.'

'Yes, I spoke to Claire about it and she said she thought so too once. She told me about Toby's mother and how neurotic she was—how she tried to teach him to play when he was little more than a baby and flew into rages when he didn't come up to her expectations.'

Sean looked up in surprise. 'Jake never told me that. But then I suppose it's understandable. It wouldn't be something he was proud of—and after the tragedy—' He looked at Katy. 'There's a tie-up here somewhere.' He stood up decisively. 'I'll ask Jake's permission now and if he agrees I'll lay on a consultation with John as soon as I can.' He stopped at the door and looked at her. 'You will come with us, won't you, Katy?'

Suddenly the traumas of the afternoon overtook her. The shock of Toby's asthma attack and near drowning, Claire's temporary laying the blame at her feet, coupled with the feeling of inadequacy she had experienced. All at once she was acutely aware of the clammy swimsuit clinging to her body. She began to shiver, hardly able to get the words past her chattering teeth.

'Yes—of course I'll come with you.'

Sean crossed the room and put his hands on her shoulders. 'Claire was right, you know. You should have a hot bath. You're shivering.'

She shook her head. 'It isn't just that. I—I feel so responsible for what happened. If Toby had—had—*died*!' She shuddered violently as the last word came out on a choking sob. The tears that would be held back no longer began to trickle down her cheeks.

'Hey—come on now, don't cry. You've been so wonderful.' Sean reached into his pocket for a handkerchief and dabbed at her tears. She looked up at him with brimming eyes.

'What would I have done though, if you hadn't arrived at that moment? The thought of it makes me go cold all over.'

'You would have coped perfectly well,' he told her firmly. 'If we're thinking like that I might well say that it was all my fault for suggesting swimming lessons for Toby in the first place.' He frowned. 'You're trembling like a leaf!' He began to rub her back and shoulders vigorously. 'Come on—into that bath. I'll run it for you.'

'Sean—' She looked up at him. 'I'm sorry for the things I said the other night—' Her voice wavered dangerously. 'You were right—I had no right to speak to you in that way.'

'You had every right. I behaved like a pompous ass!' He sighed. 'Poor little Katy. You're so mixed up, aren't you? I don't think you really know what you want, do you?'

She clamped her teeth over her lower lip to stop its trembling. 'I do, Sean—I do really. It's just that—' Before she could complete the sentence his lips closed over hers in a kiss that was slow and gentle and infinitely comforting. She relaxed against him, feeling that she would like to remain like this for ever, wrapped warmly and safely in his arms. But all too soon he was putting her gently from him.

'Katy—' He lifted her chin with one finger to look down into her eyes. 'Have that bath now and dress while I go and talk to Jake and Claire. Join us when you're ready, eh?' He smiled. 'Oh and by the way, I like the new hairstyle now that I've had time to get used to it—even if I do miss the marigold effect!'

Lying in the warm, scented bath Katy felt happier than she had for a long time. If Sean still treated her like a child, at least he seemed to have stopped despising her.

★    ★    ★

The appointment with Sean's friend, Dr John Marquand, was arranged for the following week. John lived and worked in York and when Sean told him about Toby he suggested that the three of them should meet at the Castle Museum on his day off. In showing Toby round he planned to get to know him in an informal atmosphere, then after lunch they could go back to his surgery for the consultation. Sean put the idea to Jake and Claire, who agreed and the following Wednesday saw them setting off early in the morning, an excited Toby in the back of the car.

They arrived just after ten o'clock, a little earlier than planned, and to fill in the time until they were to meet John, Sean took them for a brief sight-seeing tour round the city. Toby gazed in awe at the Minster with its twin towers, commanding the city like a great grey guardian, and at the city walls, high above their grassed banks, where one could walk and look down at the city and the river, broad and serene and silver. They went for a walk along the quaint cobbled street known as The Shambles and Toby peered, fascinated, into the little shops with their bottle-glass windows.

'Wait till you see inside the museum,' Sean told him. 'In there they've rebuilt the streets of York just as they used to be a hundred years ago—with the shops and everything. Then, down below, you can see the prison cells.'

Toby beamed in delighted anticipation.

Dr John Marquand was a slim, fair-haired man of about forty. He was waiting for them outside the museum entrance, dressed casually in a sports shirt and slacks. Toby took to him at once, especially when he learned that John had a son of about his own age.

'It's a pity he couldn't have come with us today,' he told them. 'But he and his mother have gone away for a holiday.'

The museum was an Aladdin's cave to Toby. It had everything from ancient weaponry to Victorian valentines. But, for Toby, the most fascinating of all were the reconstructed streets, correct in every detail from the cobble-stones and gas lighting to the hansom cab and the barrel organ.

Afterwards John took them all to lunch at a place reknowned for its ice-cream. Katy reflected that he certainly knew how to win a small boy's heart. John and Sean had already had a long discussion about Toby on the telephone and after the morning together they were almost like old friends.

John had decided that the best approach was a completely honest one. In his surgery the three of them sat down and John asked his receptionist to bring them some tea—orange juice for Toby. While they drank he explained carefully to Toby what he was about to try.

'Now—these nasty wheezy attacks of yours—I'm sure you'd like them to stop, wouldn't you?'

Toby nodded, looking at John over the rim of his glass. 'Arnold helps,' he said. 'I'm always better when I hold him.'

'And who might Arnold be?'

'He's my bear.' Toby looked at Katy. 'Well—Katy's bear really.'

John smiled. 'I see. And have you brought him with you today?'

Katy unzipped her bag and took Arnold out, handing him to Toby.

John looked at her approvingly. 'That's fine. He's a handsome fellow, isn't he? Well, we need all the help we can get, so I'm going to sit him up there, on top of the cupboard, where you can see each other and I want you

171

to keep an eye on him and watch that he doesn't sneak off.' John took Toby's glass from him gently. 'Now—you and Arnold are going to have a little rest because after all you've done this morning you're both rather tired.'

Toby settled himself trustingly back in the chair and Katy shot a glance towards Sean. He smiled reassuringly at her and under the cover of John's desk she felt his fingers twine round hers comfortingly.

'Just rest, Toby,' John was saying in a smooth restful voice. 'Notice how very heavy your arms and legs feel and how very comfy and warm that chair is. You've never felt so comfy and sleepy, have you, Toby. Watch Arnold. He's sleepy too. If your eyelids feel heavy just let them close. Uncle Sean and Katy and I don't mind at all.' John leaned forward towards him. 'I'm going to begin counting backwards now, Toby, starting at ten. By the time I get to one you'll be a very long way off but you will still be able to hear my voice and talk to me. Can you hear me now?' Toby nodded. He looked completely at ease. There was a smile on his face as though he were enjoying it. John began to count backwards.

'Three—two—one—Can you still hear me, Toby? You are going for a little trip now—back to when you were very small. You are three, Toby. Do you understand? How old are you?'

Toby opened his mouth, 'Three,' he whispered.

Katy bit her lip. It was uncanny, even Toby's voice had changed. He spoke with a baby lisp. Her fingers tightened involuntarily round Sean's. John continued.

'I want you to tell me about yourself, Toby. What are you doing?'

There was a long pause and for a while Katy thought it wasn't going to work, then suddenly Toby spoke.

'Daddy is taking me to the fair!' he said excitedly. 'We're having a ride on the roundabout—now we're playing the game with the little bouncy balls, Daddy says I can have a go—Ooh, I've won!'

'Well done, Toby. Did you get a prize?'

'Yes—*yes*—a shiny little fish in a plastic bag. Daddy says he'll buy me a bowl on the way home for him to live in and I can have him in my room.' Toby lapsed into silence and after a moment John asked him,

'Tell me about home, Toby—tell me about Mummy.'

Toby's eyelids flickered and he began to move restlessly in the chair. 'It's time for my piano lesson again,' he whispered. 'Mummy will be cross because I can't play the scales properly—I've tried but my hands won't reach.' His face began to crumple. 'I can't, Mummy!' he wailed pathetically. 'Please

173

don't smack me again—*please*!' Another pause, then he began to cry loudly. 'No! Don't do that! *No*—No, please don't. I'll be good—I'll practise—'

'What is Mummy doing, Toby?' John probed gently.

'It's my fish—she's pouring him away—into the thing that grinds up the rubbish. She's killing him! No! No!' Katy heard the familiar sound of wheezing and Toby's chest began to rise and fall rapidly. She half rose from her seat, a protest on her lips, then John said,

'Toby—it's all right. I won't let her do it. Your fish is quite safe now. No one can hurt it, or you either.' His voice was calm and firm. 'You're coming back now and your fish is safe and well. Do you understand?'

Toby's breathing eased, the wheezing faded. He nodded. 'Yes.'

'Rest quietly for a moment then. In a moment I shall start counting from one to ten and as I reach ten you will be eight years old again. You will be wide awake, feeling fit and well, and you won't remember anything at all about what just happened.' John allowed the boy to rest until his breathing was quiet and normal again, then he began counting—eight—nine—ten.'

Toby's eyes opened and he looked round at them. 'Have I been asleep?'

John laughed. 'I'll say you have—snoring

174

like an old grampus too! Here, have another biscuit.' Toby took one and began to munch. 'I've just thought,' John continued. 'Next time you come and see me we'll have to go to the Railway Museum, there wasn't time today. And I bet you'd like to see my son David's train set. He keeps it here at the surgery, upstairs where we have a big attic. I'll get Janet to take you up.' He rang the bell for his receptionist. 'Your Uncle Sean, Katy and I will come up and join you in a minute.'

Toby trotted off happily and John turned to them with a smile. 'Well, I think that was pretty conclusive, don't you?' He smiled at Katy. 'Perceptive of you to spot the fish aversion. I'd say that getting a new stepmother—and one who could play the piano too—triggered off his asthma again. But as he liked her so much it wasn't exactly her *personally* who caused the attacks. What happened was that she awakened earlier traumas—ones his infant mind had blocked out—the fish episode being the most disturbing.'

'Will he be cured now?' Katy asked huskily, a lump in her throat.

John shook his head. 'It will take a few more sessions and of course he may still be prone to asthma attacks for other reasons. But, if his parents are willing, I can help there by teaching him to control the symptoms.'

'I'm sure they will agree.' Sean rose to

shake hands with his friend. 'I can't tell you how grateful I am to you for giving up your one free day for us. And you've given me some fascinating material for my paper—providing of course that I have your permission to quote you?'

John nodded. 'I'm only too glad for you to do so. We're fighting a battle all the time to convince people that hypnosis is a science and not some kind of black magic.' His face broke into a mischievous smile. 'Well—shall we go upstairs now and join our young patient in a game with the train set?' He led the way, opening the door for them. 'You know I must admit to a weakness for the thing myself,' he confided. 'It wasn't altogether an accident that it came to be housed here at the surgery!'

## CHAPTER ELEVEN

From Toby's first session with John Marquand he began to improve dramatically. His attacks were mild and the intervals between them grew longer and longer. Sean was fascinated by the treatment and, apart from the days on which they took Toby to York for his treatment, Katy hardly saw him at all. Every moment of his time seemed to be spent in collating his notes and working on his paper for the medical journal.

At Bridge House the talk was all of the coming tour of the United States. Jake was to be the guest of Dave Maskell who had urged him to bring Claire and Toby along too, and now that Toby's health had improved this began to be a distinct possibility. Katy developed the feeling that she was not earning her salary—although Toby obviously enjoyed her company, there was very little to do for him.

On their final visit to John Marquand the cure of Toby's fish aversion was proved conclusively. When they arrived John opened the door to them himself.

'Come into the surgery, Toby,' he invited. 'I have a surprise present for you.'

Toby ran in ahead of them and there on the desk stood a bowl containing two large goldfish.

'David has some and I thought you might like them,' John explained. 'They're very easy to look after and they don't have to be taken for walks!'

Katy glanced at Sean and held her breath. Toby stared at the fish, mesmerised, just as he had been that day at the dentist's, then he turned to John, his face wreathed in smiles.

'Gosh, they're super—thanks! I know just what I'm going to call them—Adam and Eve.'

John opened a drawer and took out a packet of fish food. 'Here, feed them, then they'll really be yours.'

Toby happily sprinkled the food into the bowl. Still there was no sign of any wheezing and the three adults exchanged smiles.

'I did have a fish once before—a long time ago,' Toby said, frowning slightly. 'But it died. These two won't die because I shall take special care of them.'

On the way home Sean was forced to drive carefully while Toby sat in the back, his bowl of fish carefully cradled in a large cardboard box, packed with crumpled newspapers.

'I think my job here is over,' Katy said quietly, glancing at Sean's profile.

He looked at her sharply. 'What makes you say that?'

'It's obvious. Toby doesn't really need me any longer and neither do you. You have all the material you need for your work. You must have almost finished it by now anyway.'

He was silent for a moment, then he said, 'What will you do?'

She swallowed hard. 'I don't really know.'

'Have you thought about going back to St Anne's?' He looked at her. 'I'm sure they'd be happy to have you.'

She chewed her lip. 'It's rather a matter of Hobson's Choice, isn't it? Dad and Isobel won't want me and I suppose I'm too old to begin training for anything else.'

He grinned. 'Hardly, although your three years of training would be a sad waste—not to mention your undoubted skill. Anyway, I don't think you're being honest with yourself. Can you see yourself as anything other than a nurse?'

She shook her head. 'I suppose you're right.' Inwardly she was thinking that at St Anne's she would at least see Sean from time to time, even though it might only be from a distance. But the next moment even this hope was shattered.

'By the way, I've applied for a consultancy up here in Wensleydale,' he told her casually.

Her heart sank. 'Oh—when do you begin?' she asked.

'It isn't that definite—though I am on the shortlist.'

Katy stared out at the moorland scenery. Once more everything seemed to be coming to an end. These weeks at Bridge House had flown. She knew she could stay longer but she felt she really should leave. It wasn't fair to the Underwoods to hold them to the original agreement. Besides, the longer she stayed, the more painful the parting would be, when it came.

'I'll write to Mrs Bellamy tonight,' she said, referring to the St Anne's Senior Nursing Officer. 'I'll have to ask if there's a room for me at the nurses' hostel too, until I can find another flat.'

Sean smiled at her. 'That's great news. I'm sure you'll feel you've made the right decision once you've settled back there—especially

179

when you pass those finals next time round, as I'm sure you will.'

That night after dinner she gave her notice to Claire. The older woman looked thoughtful.

'Oh, Katy—this wouldn't have anything to do with Sean, would it?'

Katy was quick—a little too quick—with her denial. 'No—nothing at all. I just feel it isn't fair to you now that Toby is so much better. Jake's book is almost finished and I'm sure you'll want to spend the rest of the time together as a family before you fly off to the States.'

Claire frowned, trying to find a tactful way to ask what she was thinking. 'Forgive me for asking Katy, but is there any hope at all that you and Sean might—well—you know—get together?'

Katy shook her head, smiling ruefully. 'None at all, I'm afraid. He sees me as nothing more than a silly little nurse—at best a working acquaintance.'

Claire pursed her lips. 'I'm sure he feels more for you than that!' She could have sworn that there was more in his eyes when he looked at Katy. 'I know Sean has always been a terrible flirt but—' she broke off, looking at Katy as a sudden idea presented itself. 'How would you like to come to the States with us?'

Katy gasped, sorely tempted, but she

shook her head. 'No—thank you all the same. You don't really need me. If I'm going back to nursing the sooner the better. Besides, there's my father's wedding in September. I couldn't miss that.'

'And Sean?' Claire raised an eyebrow.

Katy shrugged. 'I shall just have to try to forget him. Once he's moved away from St Anne's it shouldn't be too hard.' She hoped she sounded more convinced than she felt.

The letter from Isobel came by first post the following morning. In it she announced that she and Katy's father were to be married sooner than they had originally planned—in ten days' time to be exact—and they both wanted Katy to come home for the wedding.

'There seems little point in wasting any more time at our age,' she wrote. 'As you know, it will be a quiet little wedding at the Register Office but it wouldn't feel right without you being there, dear. If your charming doctor friend would care to come too we would be very happy to see him. I enclose a formal invitation for you to pass on to him.'

Katy folded the letter, suppressing an exasperated little sigh. Trust Isobel to make things awkward for her again! She glanced across the breakfast table at Claire who was looking at her enquiringly.

'It's from my future stepmother,' she said. 'The wedding has been brought forward. It's to be in ten days' time.'

'Then of course you must go. Is that your invitation?' Claire nodded towards the card that lay on the table before Katy.

'No—I'm supposed to pass that on to Sean. Isobel took quite a fancy to him. She seems to have got it firmly fixed in her head that he is my boyfriend.' She picked up the card and pushed it into her pocket.

Claire leaned forward. 'You are going to give it to him though, aren't you?'

'I shall simply say that he was too busy.'

'But you can't do that! The invitation is addressed to Sean. He has a right to see it and make up his own mind.'

Katy sighed. 'You must admit it's going to make things awkward, Claire. It's embarrassing for both of us. He won't want to go anyway—he hardly knows them—yet he won't be able to refuse without looking churlish.' She shook her head. 'No—better if he knows nothing about it.'

'You're very wrong,' Claire said firmly. 'If he did have to refuse I know he would want to send a card or even a small gift. Knowing Sean as I do I'm sure he'd be furious to think he hadn't even been given the chance.' She held out her hand. 'Give me the invitation and I'll see that he gets it.'

Katy fingered the card hesitantly. 'I told you, Claire. It would make things so awkward for me. Isobel thinks we're practically engaged!'

Claire shook her head. 'You've no need to worry. It's the week that Sean has his interview. He won't want to go all the way down south, but right's right all the same.' She took the card that Katy handed her. 'I think it would be best if I posted it to him, don't you?'

The last days at Bridge House were sad ones. As she packed, Katy reflected that she had been happier here than anywhere else since her mother died. Toby followed her around, a wistful look on his face.

'It's not fair,' he remarked. 'You're only going because my asthma has got better. Would you stay if it came back?'

She ruffled his hair affectionately. 'It isn't going to come back—not ever—and just you remember that, young man.'

He sighed. 'I suppose you're going to take old Arnold away with you too?'

She laughed. 'You know, I think he feels you need him more than I do now. Maybe I'd better let him stay with you.'

Toby stared doubtfully at the bear. 'I expect I *am* really too old for a teddy, aren't I?'

'Think of him as a mascot,' Katy suggested. 'Lots of people have mascots— film stars—footballers, even pilots. Soon you'll be flying the Atlantic, you'll need Arnold then, won't you?'

He nodded eagerly. 'Gosh, that's *right*!' He looked at her thoughtfully. 'It's a pity I can't take Adam and Eve with me too. Would you look after them for me?'

She shook her head. 'I live a long way from here, Toby. And at the moment I don't even have a proper home. Why don't you ask Uncle Sean or Mrs Benson?'

He looked at her for a moment, his lower lip thrust out. 'I wish you were coming with us.'

She smiled. 'It would be nice and I'd really love it, but I have an important exam to pass.'

'Are you going to marry Uncle Sean?' he asked with a sudden candour that took her breath away.

'Whatever gave you that idea?'

He shrugged. 'I think it would be a good idea. Don't you like him then?'

She felt her cheeks growing warm. 'I like lots of people Toby, but it doesn't mean I want to marry them. Besides, I'm going all the way to Kensbridge and Uncle Sean is staying up here in Yorkshire. We shan't be seeing each other again after I leave here.' Even as she said them the words rang in her head like a funeral bell.

But Toby didn't seem to be listening. 'If you got married I could come and visit you at Raikeside Lodge in the school holidays—did you know that when we come home from America I'm going to a new school?'

184

She heaved a sigh of relief. Thank goodness he seemed to have diverted himself from that embarrassing train of thought!

Sean insisted on taking her to the station and arrived in plenty of time on Saturday morning. Claire, Jake and Toby said their goodbyes on the porch and Katy's throat was tight as she hugged them each in turn.

'I'm going to miss you all so much,' she whispered. 'Have a lovely time in America and don't forget to send me lots of postcards, Toby.'

Toby's small thin arms wound tightly round her neck, his big brown eyes bright. 'I love you, Katy,' he whispered in her ear. 'And if Uncle Sean won't marry you, I will—if you can wait till I'm grown up. In another fourteen more years I'll be as old as you!'

Katy kissed him. 'And I'll be an old lady by then.'

He clung to her until she had to disentangle the small arms from around her neck. As she climbed into the car beside Sean her eyes were wet. She fumbled in her bag for a handkerchief and Sean silently handed her his.

'This is getting to be a habit.' He looked at her briefly. 'Still, if you're sad to go it must mean that you haven't exactly been unhappy here.'

'I've *loved* it,' she sniffed. 'I've been

happier here than almost anywhere I can remember. It's all gone so quickly and I'll—I'll miss them all so much.'

'Well, you're going back to St Anne's,' he said cheerfully. 'You know plenty of people there.' He looked at her. 'You did a great job with Toby, Katy. I'm grateful to you for coming and I'm sure that the experience was useful to you too.'

She nodded. 'And rewarding.' He was talking to her as though they were on the ward again. It seemed impossible to believe what had happened that night at Raikeside Lodge on the day of the blizzard. It was almost as though it had been between two different people.

She dabbed the last tear away and handed back his handkerchief. 'You'll be coming back to St Anne's for a while at least?' she said hopefully. 'To work out the rest of your time?'

He shrugged. 'I may not. The doctor who is filling in for me seems very happy. I'm sure he'd agree to stay on and I could do with some extra time to sort things out at Raikeside Lodge.'

Her heart sank. 'But surely you'll have to come south from time to time?'

'Oh, I shall have to come down to London to talk to the editor of the medical journal.'

She looked at him, her chin lifting. 'Oh—and I suppose you'll be seeing Helen

186

Kent while you're there?'

He nodded casually, his eyes still on the road. 'I believe I did say I'd look her up.'

As he parked the car in the station car park Katy felt sick with misery. In all probability this would be the last time she saw him and she didn't know how to cope with it. He grinned at her as he hoisted her case effortlessly out of the back of the car.

'Don't look so downcast. I'm sure Jake and Claire will ask you back to Bridge House again. They like it so much that they're going to try and buy it, if the owner will agree on their price.'

Katy stood back as he bought her ticket for her at the booking office. He hadn't the least idea of how she felt and probably would only have laughed and made a joke of it if he had. She thought of the work that lay ahead of her in the coming weeks and was glad. She was going to need her every moment occupied if she was to put him out of her mind. She glanced at her watch. It was almost time for the train. There wouldn't even be time for a cup of coffee together.

The station announcer's voice came over the public address system with its usual nasal drone: 'The train now arriving at platform two is the ten-five for London, King's Cross. Passengers for—'

She looked up at Sean but before she had time to speak his arms went round her and he was kissing her hard.

'Goodbye, little marigold,' he whispered against her hair. 'Work hard and pass that exam. Take care of yourself.' He bundled her into the train and stood back, waving as it drew out of the station.

Katy stood forlornly at the window for a long time, tears standing in her eyes and her throat aching with all the words that would never be said. Rows of houses gave way to moorland, fields and trees, each mile taking her further away from Sean—and from the impossible dream in her heart. Now it was time to wake up to cold reality, to go back and face her failures—to try to begin all over again.

## CHAPTER TWELVE

Katy sat in the bus on her way back to Kensbridge. On her lap was a large bag containing the outfit she had just bought for the wedding: a two-piece in soft, cream silk and a wide-brimmed picture hat trimmed with forget-me-nots. She had come to town to keep her appointment with Mrs Bellamy, the Senior Nursing Officer at St Anne's. Everything had been arranged. She was to start back on the wards on Monday next and there was a room vacant for her at the nurses' hostel—she had been lucky, she was told. She had gone to look at it and come away depressed at its smallness after the spacious room she had grown used to at Bridge House. Some of the newer teaching hospitals had trim little flats for two or more nurses to share—not so St Anne's, built in the early part of the century. She hoped she would soon be lucky enough to find other accommodation that she could make more home-like.

At Cremorne Crescent Isobel had been busy making changes. Katy's old bedroom had been redecorated and refurnished and now awaited its new occupants, so Katy had been relegated to the box-room until after the wedding. Her father seemed to be in a daze and more vague than ever, whilst Isobel whirled around in her element—ordering flowers, arranging the catering and attending to a hundred and one other things. What had been originally intended as a 'quiet little wedding' had assumed the proportions of a state occasion, or so it seemed to Katy.

Mrs Bellamy had been pleased to see her again and glad that she had changed her mind about giving up nursing. She conceded that caring for Toby had been useful experience, but not, in her view, as good as staying on at St Anne's would have been. However, she agreed that Katy should take her finals again at the next sitting.

189

'It will mean a concentrated effort on your part,' she warned. 'Though I feel confident that you will succeed this time.'

The bus stopped at the corner of Cremorne Crescent and Katy got off, walking along the familiar tree-lined road. Tomorrow Isobel would become Mrs Lang and after a brief honeymoon she would be moving in with Dad. She seemed to have unearthed a huge pile of Katy's belongings whilst reorganising the house. As soon as the wedding was over she would have to set about the task of sorting through them. Katy sighed. The miniscule room at the nurses' hostel would hold only the minimum. It looked as though she would soon be making another trip to the charity shop. 'I might as well go and live at the place,' she told herself as she opened the front gate. 'Soon I'll feel more at home there than anywhere else!'

The great day dawned bright and sunny. Katy rose early and made her father's breakfast, reflecting that it would be for the last time. He ate it calmly and when Katy asked him if there was anything she could do to help him get ready he shook his head. Putting down his knife and fork he looked at her.

'There is one thing I'd like you to do, Katy,' he said. 'Will you go over to Isobel and ask if you can help her—make a little gesture.' He smiled his half-shy smile. 'She

190

wants very badly to be your friend, you know.'

Katy shook her head. 'She might think I was interfering, Dad. I feel in the way as it is.'

He reached across the table to touch her hand. 'Isobel feels that you resent her. I've told her a dozen times it isn't so but she won't listen—says she'd feel the same in your place. I wish you'd go across and try to put things straight. It'd be the nicest wedding present you could give me.'

She smiled at him, feeling a little guilty. Had she really allowed her feelings to show that much? Dad was always so quiet, one tended to think he didn't notice. 'All right, Dad. I'll go now. But do go up and make a start, won't you? You don't want to keep Isobel waiting at the Register Office.'

Isobel answered her knock at the door looking pale and slightly tearful. She seemed taken aback to see Katy standing outside. 'Oh—come in, dear.'

Katy looked at her with concern. 'Is anything wrong? Don't you feel well?'

To her dismay Isobel burst into tears. 'I'm sorry, dear,' she sniffed. 'With all there's been to do I haven't really thought about it but last night it all sort of came over me!'

Katy stared at her. 'You're not having second thoughts about Dad, are you?'

Isobel bit her lip, shaking her head hard.

'No—not about David. It's you! I feel I'm taking so much from you—your father, your home. I was so carried away with my own good luck, when I met David it all seemed so wonderful—too good to be true, almost. Even when I first met you I didn't give you much thought, you had your job and your own friends. But since you came back from Yorkshire I've seen another side of you—a side that made me wonder.'

Katy took her hand and pressed it. 'You're not to let thoughts like this spoil your big day,' she said firmly. 'Don't worry about me. I have a lot of work to get down to over the coming weeks. It wouldn't be possible for me to live at home anyway.'

Isobel looked at her, still not quite convinced. 'When I met that nice young doctor of yours I thought—but then when I got the letter I could see that it wasn't as I'd imagined—and when I think of the way I must have embarrassed you!' She bit her lip in anguish.

Katy swallowed hard. 'Letter—you had a letter—from Sean?'

'To say he didn't think he would be able to make the wedding—that he was taking a job up there in Yorkshire. Well—I knew from that that you and he couldn't be close. Either that or you'd quarrelled.'

Katy shook her head. 'Don't worry about that. It's all in the past now. Today we're all making a new start and you can't begin it with tears on your face. Here—let me help you get ready. You don't want to keep Dad waiting, do you?'

Isobel hugged her, smiling now. 'Bless you, Katy. We will have a good relationship, you and I. I'll never take your mother's place—I wouldn't be fool enough to try, but I would like to be your friend and to feel I was someone you can come to.' She laughed nervously as she hurried into the bedroom. 'My trouble is that I talk too much when I get nervous. I say silly things and put my foot in it, but you'll get used to me.'

When she was dressed in the pretty delphinium-blue dress and hat, Katy left her sipping a small glass of brandy for courage whilst she went across to change herself. She found her father pacing the landing and looking nervous for the first time. She hugged him reassuringly.

'Dad—you're a very lucky man,' she told him. 'Isobel looks beautiful. We've had a long talk and I think we understand each other a whole lot better now.'

He looked relieved. 'That's good news.' He looked at her. 'Hadn't you better start getting yourself ready? The cars will be here soon and you don't want to keep us waiting, do you?'

Katy stared at him for a moment, then burst into a peal of laughter. 'I seem to have heard those words somewhere else this morning!' she told him.

After the private ceremony at the Register Office a reception was being held at the Park View Hotel and Katy was surprised at the number of guests who arrived. The newly-weds looked happy and relaxed now that the ceremony was over. They had eyes only for each other and Katy tried to perform the duties normally carried out by the bride's mother—circulating among the guests to make sure that they all had something to eat and drink and that strangers were introduced to each other. The cake was cut and telegrams read. Toasts were drunk and speeches were made, after which the guests began to wander out through the open french windows on to the hotel lawn to stand chatting in groups.

Katy looked around her with a sigh. Soon it would all be over. Dad and Isobel would be leaving for Torquay and she would be faced with the prospect of a lonely weekend—just her and the pile of accumulated rubbish in the box-room. The air was warm and heavy as she wandered out on to the terrace and began to cross the lawn towards the car park, looking for a quiet place to cool down. Halfway, she felt a drop of rain on her cheek—then another and another. She darted for the shelter of a clump of trees but as she did so there was a brilliant flash of lightning followed by an earsplitting crash of thunder that brought a cry of alarm to her lips. She withdrew further under the trees, knowing full well that it was the last place she should be sheltering in a thunderstorm. Why hadn't she dashed towards the hotel when she felt the rain starting? If she made a run for it now her beautiful new suit and hat would be ruined. Crossly she pulled off her hat and shook the raindrops from it, watching as the rain pattered down and the rest of the wedding guests fled indoors. She pushed a hand through her hair, wondering how long it would be before she could join them.

'You look like a marigold in a thunderstorm!'

She spun round with a squeak of surprise. 'Sean! What are you doing here?'

He grinned at her. 'Asking to be struck by lightning, like you! I *was* invited to the wedding you know.'

'I—I know—but—'

'Don't tell me I'm too late! Is it all over?'

'No—no—it isn't over—' She was staring at him, her heart beating so fast that she could hardly breathe. Here he was, standing close to her and looking down into her eyes with that familiar amused look she always found so devastating. Somehow, all she wanted to say seemed to dry on her tongue.

'You know, I was wrong,' he said stepping closer. 'You're not a marigold any more Katy, and it isn't just the hair.' He put out one finger to catch a raindrop that was about to slide down her cheek. 'You're more like a tiger-lily.'

'I—thought you couldn't come,' she said in a whisper. 'I thought we'd said goodbye for the last time.'

He smiled gently. 'So did I. I told myself that it was for the best, that I could forget you—that I *should* forget you—but as you see, I couldn't stay away.' His hands were on her shoulders and she was acutely aware of his touch—of the warmth of his fingers through the thin material of her dress.

'Over these past weeks I've felt so many things for you, Katy—admiration, irritation, *exasperation*—but I finally had to admit that it all added up to one feeling in the end.' He pulled her close. 'I'm in love with you—that's what I'm really trying to say. In love with you—to stay.'

She opened her mouth to speak but he went on, 'I know I'm twelve years older than you and that you don't approve of age gaps—I even told myself that it was probably a father figure you were looking for and that you should be left alone to sort your mixed-up feelings out.' He smiled wryly, shaking his head. 'But none of it was any use. I'm just too damned selfish. I want you too much to care any longer. When I woke up this morning I knew it was my last chance, so I jumped into the car and here I am—at your mercy. Now you can tell me to get lost if you want to.'

She stared up at him incredulously, shaking her head. 'Oh, Sean—I don't understand half of what you're saying—but I am glad you're here.' She wound her arms round his neck and pressed her face against his shoulder. 'I tried not to fall in love with you too—but not for the reasons you think. If you only knew how much it hurt to say goodbye.'

He lifted her chin with one finger and kissed her. 'There isn't a thing you can tell me about that. But I warn you—you're going to be seeing quite a lot of me in the future. I don't intend to let you out of my sight again in a hurry!'

'But your new job?' She looked up at him. 'And I'm starting back at St Anne's again on Monday.'

'So am I!' He grinned. 'I took myself off the shortlist for the new job. Until a certain staff nurse can come with me I'm not moving. And now, if you wouldn't mind shutting up for five minutes, I'd rather like to kiss you properly!'

He crushed her close and she gave herself up to the heady delight of his kisses till her head reeled, she pushed him gently away, laughing breathlessly.

'Sean—we're forgetting about the wedding! Dad and Isobel will be leaving soon and you haven't seen them! They'll be wondering where on earth I've got to.'

He caught her hand and turned it over, kissing the palm. 'In just a moment. I haven't said what I drove all these miles to say yet. Will you marry me, Katy?'

She looked at him for a long moment, her eyes misty. 'Oh, Sean!'

He bit the tip of her little finger. 'Well—come on—are you going to put me out of my misery? Is it yes or no?'

'It's yes, of course!' She stood on tiptoe to kiss him, her heart almost bursting with happiness. 'To think that when I woke up this morning—' But the rest of her words were lost as his lips found hers again in a kiss that told her all she ever dreamed of knowing about what he felt for her.

It was some time before they moved again. Under the dripping branches it was as though they hung together in space, oblivious to the dying storm and the rest of the world around them. At last, voices from the car park brought them back to reality.

'Dad and Isobel must be leaving for their honeymoon!' Katy said, catching at Sean's hand. 'Come on, we'd better run or we'll miss them!'

The rain had stopped and as they ran across the lawn to the car park they were just in time to see David and Isobel Lang getting into their car. Isobel pointed.

198

'Here she is—here's Katy!'

'Look who arrived—almost too late,' Katy said breathlessly.

'Congratulations!' Sean shook hands with them both. 'I'm glad I was at least in time to see you before you left.' He cleared his throat. 'I don't know if this is an appropriate moment or not, but I'd like to ask for permission to marry your daughter, Mr Lang.'

Later, as they watched the car out of sight, Katy laughed. 'Dad's face! I'm sure that was the last piece of news he expected today.' She slipped her arm happily through Sean's.

He looked down at her. 'What were you planning to do with this weekend?' he asked.

She smiled ruefully. 'Clear out the box-room, believe it or not! Sounds madly exciting, doesn't it?'

He bent to kiss her, teasing her with his eyes. 'I'd say it had distinct possibilities. Is the box-room big enough for two?'

She nodded, laughing. 'A tight squeeze, I'd say.'

'Then I suggest we make a start as soon as possible,' he said. 'I've a feeling that it's going to take us quite a long time!'

Photoset, printed and bound in Great Britain by REDWOOD PRESS LIMITED, Melksham, Wiltshire